MATT DIXON SWORE HE'D KILL HIS FATHER

—if he ever found out who he was.

Matt made no secret of his hatred for the father who ran off and deserted a young, attractive wife, an infant son and a mortgaged farm. No matter that Ephraim Dixon was wrongly accused of murder and made his getaway while he could.

Matt Dixon had an old daguerrotype to go by in his manhunt. It wasn't much, but he knew he'd recognize the coward by those eyes. Matt knew he wouldn't say much to the old man either. Just squeeze the trigger. . . .

We will send you a free catalog on request. Any titles not in your local book store can be purchased by mail. Send the price of the book plus 50¢ shipping charge to Tower Books, P.O. Box 270, Norwalk, Connecticut 06852.

Titles currently in print are available for industrial and sales promotion at reduced rates. Address inquiries to Tower Publications, Inc., Two Park Avenue, New York, New York 10016, Attention: Premium Sales Department.

THE COLORADO GUN

Edwin Booth

TOWER BOOKS NEW YORK CITY

A TOWER BOOK

Published by

Tower Publications, Inc.
Two Park Avenue
New York, N.Y. 10016

Copyright © 1981 by Edwin Booth

All rights reserved
Printed in the United States

Chapter One

The stranger's gun spat flame, and Matt felt a tug at his left arm. Then his own gun roared, and the stranger, a surprised look on his face, crumpled to the floor, pistol slipping from suddenly lifeless fingers.

Before the echo of the shots faded, there was the pound of running feet in the street, and a man's voice called sharply from the darkness outside the batwings, "You're covered, all of you, so don't try anything! You, there by the bar, lay down your gun and move away from it!"

Still dazed by the abruptness of what had happened, Matt laid his gun on the damp wood and edged out of reach. At this, the batwings were pushed apart, and a tall, gray-haired man came into the saloon. He had a cocked sixgun in his hand, and there was a marshal's star pinned to his vest. His eyes flicked from Matt to the motionless man on the floor, rested briefly on the only other visible occupant of the room, and then he asked of no one in particular, "What's going on here?"

This brought the bartender into sight from behind the bar, where he had ducked when the shooting started. His round, bald head glistened with sweat, and he made two false starts before managing to say, "Search me, Marshal. Everything was peaceful when I went in the back room with some empty bottles. Whatever started, it happened while I was gone."

The marshal slanted a glance at the downed man, looked at the other, who was just beginning to show signs of recovering from shock, and apparently decided that if he were to get a sensible explanation, it would have to be from the one whose arm was bleeding.

"How about it, mister? As a start, what's your name?"

"Dixon," Matt said, turning to face the marshal squarely, and trying to keep his voice steady. He had never before killed anyone in his twenty-one years, and reaction was setting in.

"All right, Dixon," the marshal said. "Let's hear your side of the story."

Matt took a quick look at the man he had killed, suppressed a shudder, and focused his attention on the marshal.

"I'm almost as much in the dark as you are, Marshal. I rode into town an hour ago, tied my horse out front, and came in for a drink. A drink, and to ask the bartender the same question I've been putting to everyone else I've met in the last year, whether he knew a man by the name of Ephraim Dixon. The bartender said he didn't, but when he went into the back room, that one. . ." he pointed at the dead man. . . "asked why I wanted to know. He was sort of nasty about it, and I felt like telling him it was none of his business, but on the chance he might be able to give me a lead, I held my temper, and told him that Ephraim Dixon was my father."

"Keep talking," the marshal prompted, when Matt paused. "There must be more to it than that."

"Yes," Matt acknowledged. "He said something like, ~~————————————~~ What makes you think he might be around here?' Well, I was mad by then, so I told him ~~————~~. He drew his gun, and winged me while I was bringing my own into line, but before he could try again, I shot him. Killed him, I guess, from the looks of things."

The marshal frowned, and turned to look at the other man, who had recovered, and was glowering at Matt.

"Have you got anything to add, stranger? And just to keep the record straight, what's your name?"

"Quigley," the fellow muttered. "That's my brother Kelso lying there dead. This feller. . ." he pointed at Matt. "This feller's old man killed our other brother, name of Luke. That was a long time ago, but Kelso and me have been looking for him ever since. It's a lie about Kelso shooting first. He was just protecting himself."

The marshal frowned at him in disgust.

"That's hogwash and you know it. Your brother couldn't possibly have pulled the trigger after that bullet slammed into his chest, and I heard only two shots. Your brother started it, didn't he?"

Quigley didn't say anything, but his silence was answer enough. The marshal returned his attention to Matt.

"Looks like you're in the clear, Dixon. How about this other one? Did he take any part in it?"

"No," Matt said. "It seemed like he didn't realize what was going on until his brother was down, and by then I had him covered. So far as I'm concerned, you can let him go. After I ask him one question, that is." He looked at Quigley, who was scowling at him.

"You said you and your brother had been looking for my father. Was there any reason to think he might be here in Colorado?"

The man shook his head.

"No, that had nothing to do with us being here."

Matt's disappointment was short-lived. He had followed so many false leads in the past year that he was used to failure. He turned back to the bar, picked up the glass of whiskey he had been about to drink before Kelso Quigley's interruption, and sipped it slowly. Behind him, the marshal said, "All right, Quigley, or whatever your real name is. You can take your brother along and bury him, or leave him here and I'll see he gets planted in Boot Hill. Either way, I want you out of town inside the hour, and if I ever see you here in Colbyville again you'll be in deep trouble. Savvy?"

Quigley nodded, took a last look at his dead brother, and hurried out of the saloon. There was the creak of saddle leather, followed by the pound of hoofs, and the marshal moved up beside Matt and signalled for a drink. When both men had emptied their glasses, he said mildly, "Since nobody else has showed up, I reckon it leaves the burying up to me. Do you feel like giving me a hand, or is your arm bothering you too much?''

Matt didn't relish the idea, but the marshal had treated him fairly, so he could hardly refuse. He picked up his gun and holstered it, and between them they dragged Kelso's body out of the saloon, draped it across his horse, which the younger brother had foolishly failed to take with him, and headed for the graveyard. By the light of the stars, and using shovels which the marshal got from a small tool shed, they scraped out a shallow grave. After the marshal went through the dead man's pockets without finding anything of significance, they rolled the body into the grave, covered it with dirt, and then each of them made a cigarette and lit it. Through the smoke, the marshal looked at Matt and commented, "Seems like somebody should've said a few words, but the man was a stranger to me. I guess he'll get wherever he's going without any speeches. Come over to my office and wash up. There's coffee on the stove, and we'll talk. Maybe I can help you find your pa. If not, I can at least take a look at your arm.''

Matt nodded his agreement. He didn't anticipate that the marshal would be of much help, but the prospect of hot coffee was pleasing. Besides, he doubted that he could go to sleep easily, after having just killed a man. He walked beside the marshal, who was leading the dead man's horse, waited while the animal was stabled, then followed the marshal into his little office. A coal-oil lamp was burning on the desk, and by its murky light, Matt could see the barred door of a single cell at the back of the room. At the marshal's suggestion, he took off his brush jacket and shirt, and sat down on a straight-backed chair which, together with the desk and a swivel chair, constituted the room's furnishings.

The marshal bent down for a closer look at Matt's arm, and grunted with satisfaction.

"Nothing to worry about, Dixon. I'll wash it out if you say so, but chances are it'd do more harm than good. By the way, my name's Freeman, Ike Freeman."

Matt saw no need to comment, so he merely nodded, and watched the marshal go behind the desk and settle down with a sigh in the swivel chair. For a few minutes it seemed that the marshal had forgotten why Matt had come with him, then he broke the silence by saying, "This father of yours, Ephraim Dixon, what made you think he might be here in Colbyville?"

"Nothing," Matt said and, at the marshal's puzzled look, "It's just a place to look, like a thousand others. I didn't expect to bump into the Quigleys, of course, although I've heard of them from time to time."

"Nothing good, I bet," the marshal surmised. "But go on with your story. How long has your pa been missing?"

"Twenty years," Matt said, and had to smile at the marshal's expression. "I was only a baby when he disappeared. Too small to remember him."

"And how long have you been looking for him?"

"About sixteen months. I didn't start until my mother died. That was a year ago last April. In Indiana. I couldn't get away sooner, because she hasn't been well for several years, and I've been taking care of her. Farm work, mostly, ever since I was old enough to milk a cow."

The marshal frowned.

"For a ploughboy, you seem to be pretty handy with a sixgun. That feller you shot was a stranger to me, but from the way he wore his holster, I'd say he was a gunslinger. How'd you manage to outgun him?"

"There was a farm hand I worked with back in Indiana. If he was still alive, I wouldn't tell you who he was, because I've an idea he was wanted for something out here in the west, but since he's dead, I guess there's no harm mentioning his name. It was Jake Huggins. He taught me all I know about shooting."

"Jake Huggins!" the marshal exclaimed. "So *that's* where he's been hiding out. Well, I'll say this, you had a good teacher. Jake knew everything there was to know about handguns. But let's hear the rest of it."

"That's all there is," Matt said. His arm was beginning to hurt, and he wanted to go somewhere and lie down. "Except that if you know anything about my father, I'd appreciate your telling me. Here's what he looked like twenty-one years ago." He took a faded daguerrotype from his pocket and held it out.

The marshal studied the picture, which was of a rather handsome, smooth-shaven man, handed it back, and got up to fill two cups with coffee from a pot on the small stove. He gave one to Matt, who accepted it with thanks, then went back to his own chair behind the desk and said thoughtfully, "The name Dixon doesn't mean anything to me, nor does the picture. Which doesn't prove much, being as every third man you meet around here is using a name he didn't start out with. Especially if he's on the run. Would your pa. . . ?"

"Be running from something?" Matt finished, and shrugged. "Maybe not now, but he was at first. You already heard about it over at the saloon. He killed the older brother of those two Quigleys. Before the law could come and ask him about it, he lit a shuck. I guess he couldn't face the idea of being penned up. The funny thing is that if he'd waited, he most likely wouldn't have had to go to jail. Luke Quigley, from what I've heard since, was a no-good troublemaker. No jury would have convicted my father for doing what he did, being as Quigley had spread some bad lies about my mother."

"But your pa spooked," the marshal said. "It's happened before. I suppose you're looking for him to tell him he's in the clear."

"No," Matt said, and could feel his face muscles tightening. "When I find him, I'm going to kill him!"

Chapter Two

At about the time that Matt Dixon and the Colbyville town marshal were burying Kelso Quigley's mortal remains, another lawman, this one wearing a star engraved with the title "Sheriff," was making his last nightly rounds of the business section of Holbrook, Arizona, rattling doors to make sure they were locked, while keeping a sharp lookout for anything out of line.

To the citizens of Holbrook, and to ranchers in the area, his name was presumed to be Durham. It said something of his character that after ten years in town, first as a deputy, and more recently as sheriff, only one person, Ellen Troup, called him by his first name, Ed, and she only when they were alone.

Not that the sheriff was disliked, for he wasn't, as attested to by his being re-elected every year. He was respected, too, even by those renegades whose illegal activities were curtailed by his presence. Newcomers to town were warned that Holbrook wasn't a good place in which to start trouble.

It was rather ironic that the only person who called him Ed was also the only one who knew that his real name was Ephraim Dixon. In a unguarded moment, he had told Ellen the whole story, how he had killed a man back in Indiana, then panicked and abandoned his wife and infant son rather than face imprisonment.

Ellen, who owned and operated the town's only restaurant, was not inclined to pass judgement on others. She had listened quietly to the sheriff's account of what had happened in Indiana, but had offered neither sympathy nor censure. She could sense that the sheriff had been punishing himself all these years, which probably accounted for his reserved attitude, and for his looking older than his actual forty-one years.

It was not unusual for the sheriff to pay Ellen a visit after completing his nightly rounds. In a place the size of Holbrook, this could hardly go unnoticed. To the men of the town it was only natural, and except for admiring his taste, they gave it little thought. As for the town's womenfolk, whose standards of morality were somewhat more strict, they had learned to accept it. Most of them liked Ellen, though this feelng was mixed with envy because of her good looks. At any rate, they were wise enough to know that there was nothing they could do to change the situation.

On this particular night, Ellen was watching from the front window of her darkened bedroom, which was an extension of the cafe. Her eyes followed the sheriff's progress as he pursued his nightly routine, and she smiled with pleasure when he finished his tour and headed for the restaurant, which had been closed for several hours. She left the bedroom, entered the restaurant through a connecting doorway, and let him in without waiting for him to knock.

Neither of them spoke until they were in the bedroom, the window shades drawn, and a lamp lit.

It was unmistakably a woman's room, but without many frills or furbelows. Clean, white curtains hung at the two windows, one of which faced the street, the other, at a ninety degree angle, looking out on a vacant lot beyond which, some thirty feet away, was the blank wall of the saloon. A neatly made double bed with a hand crocheted spread stood against the back wall, and next to it was a dresser with attached mirror. A straight-backed chair was in front of the dresser. There was also a larger, more comfortable chair near the side window, and it was toward this that Ellen nodded, as she said in her rather low-pitched voice, "Sit down, Ed, while I get us some coffee." Almost as an afterthought, she added, "You look troubled. Is something wrong?"

The sheriff shook his head, and some of the harshness left his face. He even managed a smile as he said, "No, everything's quiet. A cup of coffee would taste good, though, and I won't mind getting the weight off my feet."

Ellen, who knew him so well, wasn't entirely satisfied with his answer. Something was worrying him, despite his denial. She didn't press the point, however, but went back into the restaurant, leaving the door open to provide enough light so that she could see to fill two cups from the large coffeepot which had been kept warm by the embers of the suppertime fire. Since neither she nor the sheriff used cream or sugar, she carried the two cups into the bedroom, handed one to the sheriff, then turned and closed the door.

For a few minutes neither of them spoke. It was a companionable silence, the sheriff, in his chair, slowly unwinding as he was warmed by the coffee, Ellen standing near the front window, waiting for him to break the spell.

He did, finally, saying soberly, "What I just said about everything being quiet is true. You're right, though; something's on my mind. Today would have been Nora's and my twenty-third wedding anniversary."

Ellen's hand, holding the cup, twitched ever so slightly, but not enough to spill any of the contents. It was one of the few times the name Nora had been mentioned, and she hadn't been prepared for it. Controlling her voice with an effort, she said matter-of-factly, "It's only natural, I suppose, for you to remember, but thinking about it isn't going to do any good. Especially since. . . " She hesitated.

"Since she's dead?" the sheriff said. Word of his wife's death had reached him in a roundabout fashion several months before. "You're right, of course. There's nothing I can do for her now. Not," he added wryly, "that I did anything while I could have." He was silent for a long moment, then added musingly, "I wonder about the boy Matt."

"Boy?" Ellen repeated. "He'd be a man by now, and well able to take care of himself. He surely can't remember you. Didn't you say he was less than two years old when. . . when it happened?"

"That's right," the sheriff agreed. "Like as not

he's got more important things to think about than a good-for-nothing pa who ran out." He made an impatient gesture, and added apologetically, "I'm miserable company tonight. Shouldn't have bothered you with my troubles. Let's have some more of your good coffee and forget it." He held out his empty cup.

When Ellen returned with the fresh coffee, she saw that the sheriff had unbuckled his gunbelt and laid it and the holstered gun on the floor. She thought about it a moment, then said mildly, "I think when we finish your coffee you'd better leave."

The sheriff looked up quickly, his eyes troubled. "Did I say something I shouldn't? I didn't mean. . . "

"It isn't that," Ellen said, shaking her head. "But tonight. . . well, it wouldn't be right, somehow. I think you understand."

The sheriff studied her expression a long time, sighed, and reached down for his gunbelt. He stood up, strapped the belt around his waist, and said reluctantly, "I reckon you're right. You generally are. Are things the same? Between us, I mean?"

"Of course," Ellen said, smiling. "And tomorrow we'll forget all about this conversation. Agreed?"

"Agreed," the sheriff said, relieved by her tone. "Thanks for the coffee."

"You're welcome," Ellen told him. "Take care of yourself until I see you."

"Don't I always?" the sheriff asked. He made no move to take her in his arms, although he wanted to, but left the restaurant, listened to make sure she had bolted the door after him, then headed for his modest house at the other end of the street.

Perhaps because he was so preoccupied with his thoughts, it came as a complete surprise when there was a loud explosion from the vicinity of the bank.

Instantly alert, he headed that direction on the run, at the same time drawing his revolver. As he neared the bank, a man burst out the front door, one hand clutching a canvas bag, which could be presumed to contain money. He vaulted into the saddle of a waiting horse, and took off at a gallop.

The sheriff set himself, took careful aim, holding his gun in both hands, and squeezed the trigger. Despite the faint light and moving target, his aim was good. The rider let out a yell, flung up his arms, lost his grip on the moneybag, and fell out of the saddle, to lie sprawled in the road.

The sheriff approached warily, thinking the man might be playing possum. He had come close enough to kick the fellow's gun out of reach, when a sound behind him made him turn his head. A second man was coming out of the bank, his gun fisted. Before the sheriff could finish turning, the man's gun barked. Something slammed into the sheriff's left leg, which collapsed under him, pitching him on top of the man he had shot. The fall jolted his gun out of his hand, and by the time he had recovered it, the second robber had mounted and ridden out of range.

Lamps began to come on in the nearby houses, and a voice which the sheriff recognized as that of Rex Bates, the town banker, demanded sharply,

"What the devil's going on out here?"

"Your bank's been robbed," the sheriff called. "One of the men got away. The other one's dead."

"Good God!" Bates shouted, as he raced toward the bank.

By then several other townsmen, in various stages of undress, had reached the street. One of them said excitedly, "Here's a moneybag. Cripes! It's full of dough!"

The sheriff felt foolish, sitting on the ground amid a growing cluster of curious townsmen. He tried to get up, and when his left leg wouldn't support him, said rather hotly, "Don't just stand there, damn it! If you get a move on, you might catch the fellow who got away. Meanwhile, I could use a little help getting over to Doc Yarborough's."

Three or four of the men hurried away, presumably to get guns and to saddle their horses. As they did, the sheriff's young deputy, Al Gregg, pushed his way through the rest of the group. He had taken time to dress, and the sheriff's first impulse was to upbraid him for being so slow. On second thought, he admitted to himself that Gregg had acted properly. He, alone of the crowd, was ready to ride. The sheriff brushed aside the hands which were going to help him up, and said to Gregg, "One man lit out, headed south. He's riding an Appaloosa, so you'll have no trouble recognizing him. Get going!"

"Yes, sir," Al Gregg said, and took off at a trot. By the time the sheriff had been helped up and was standing on his one good leg, there was the sound of a galloping horse headed in the direction taken by the escaping robber.

Doc Yarborough, a man of about the sheriff's age, was possessed of an unshakable composure. An Easterner who had come west for his health, leaving behind an important position in a Baltimore hospital, he wasted no time regretting what some might have considered a foul stroke of fate. Nor did he waste time pronouncing his verdict on the sheriff's injured leg.

"You'll be doing no walking without crutches for at least a month, Sheriff. The bullet didn't do too much damage, but you must have twisted your leg when you fell. Anyway, you've got a fractured tibia, shinbone in layman's language. Fortunately for you, neither part of the bone punctured the skin. I'll put splints on it, but the first order of business is to set it properly. It's going to hurt like the devil. Do you want me to give you something to knock you out?"

The sheriff was silent as he tried to absorb the full implications of what Doc Yarborough had said. A sheriff who had to use crutches was little better than no sheriff at all. He took a deep breath, and asked bluntly, "What about later on? Will the leg be any good again?"

"It should be," the doctor said. "Barring complications, and assuming that you follow my orders, chances are it'll be as good as new. But we're wasting time, and you haven't answered my question."

"Forget about putting me to sleep," the sheriff said. "Let's get it over with."

The doctor nodded, and beckoned to three men out of the group whose curiosity had led them into his office.

"He's going to buck like a colt. Two of you hold his shoulders, the other clamp onto his good leg. I don't relish getting kicked."

There was a stir in the crowd, and Ellen Troup moved up to look worriedly at the sheriff, then at the doctor. "Is there anything I can do?"

Before Doc Yarborough could answer, the sheriff said drily, "Just one thing. You can go far enough away so as not to hear me when I start to yell. I've a notion I may use words not fit for a lady's ears." He forced a grin, and added, "Okay?"

Ellen tried to match his grin, failed, and hurried off. The doctor gave her time to get away, then motioned for the three men to take over their duties. When they were ready, he took hold of the sheriff's left foot, braced himself, and pulled.

The sheriff's warning to Ellen had been unnecessary. Instead of swearing, he passed out. When he came to, he had been moved onto a cot which the doctor kept for just such emergencies. His left leg was on fire, and his head was splitting, but through a haze, he could see the doctor smiling down at him. How the hell could anyone smile at a time like this?

If Doc Yarborough could read minds, he wasn't in the least disconcerted. He said cheerfully, "You were lucky, Sheriff. The bone popped right back into place. You can be thankful it wasn't a compound fracture. By the way, Ellen Troup has been here half a dozen times. Oh, incidentally, all the bank's money was in the bag that fellow dropped. Rex Bates is walking on air."

The sheriff moistened his lips and said hoarsely, "I couldn't care less about Rex Bates and his money. If he'd listened to me and bought a decent safe five years ago, this wouldn't have happened. Did my deputy catch up with the other crook?"

"No," the doctor said. "He found the Appaloosa, all right, only the fellow had evidently switched horses. But about Miss Troup. She'll probably be back soon. Do you want to see her?"

The sheriff had to think about this a minute. There was no one he would *rather* see, but first he wanted time to straighten out a few things in his mind. Since learning of Nora's death, he had been working up his courage to ask Ellen to marry him. Now it wouldn't be fair. The county wasn't likely to keep paying a sheriff who was incapable of performing his duties. The taxpayers might be sympathetic, but they were also tight fisted. He shook his head.

"Tell her I'm not up to seeing anybody yet, Doc. Maybe in a day or so."

The doctor shrugged.

"Whatever you say, Sheriff, but if you want an unsolicited opinion, I think you're making a mistake. If someone like Ellen Troup wanted to see *me*, I sure wouldn't keep her waiting."

"Since it's my mistake, suppose you let me worry about it," the sheriff said curtly, and the doctor left the room, after which the sheriff stared bleakly at the ceiling and cursed himself for being a fool.

Chapter Three

Matt, having blurted out his determination to kill his father, expected some protest from the Colbyville town marshal. He was prepared to defend his position by telling how his mother, left with a mortgaged farm which she was not qualified to run, and with an infant son to care for, had lost the farm and been forced to accept menial labor in town; how she had gone downhill physically, and yet had somehow managed to keep working until he, Matt, had been big enough to take over. He would also tell the marshal how his mother, a young and attractive woman at the time of her abandonment, had steadfastly repulsed the advances of men who had tried to persuade her to get a divorce and re-marry.

Somewhat to Matt's disappointment, he was given no opportunity to present his case. The marshal, after a prolonged silence, said merely, "It's late, and you must be tired. If you've got no better place to bed down, you're welcome to use the bunk back there in the cell. Providing you don't mind sleeping in a jail, that is."

The offer was made with a smile, and Matt, though he felt let down, matched it with one of his own.

"I've slept in worse places, Marshal, and you're right about my being tired. I'm obliged to you."

"See you in the morning, then," the marshal said, and got out of his chair. "My house is out back, in case anyone needs me for anything. I'll stable your horse. Better bolt the door after I leave. That Quigley feller might still be hanging around."

Matt nodded, and after the marshal had left, slid the bolt on the office door. He didn't really expect any trouble from Quigley; his main reason for bolting the door was that he didn't want anyone to come in and lock him in the cell. He had an almost morbid dread of being confined. It was as close as he could come to understanding why his father had taken flight rather than risk being jailed.

As it turned out, Matt didn't see the marshal again. He awoke before sunrise, as was his habit, went to the marshal's stable, where he quietly saddled his horse, and rode out of town without disturbing anyone. By the time the sun came up, he had put a good five miles between himself and Colbyville. He came to a small stream, dismounted, fed his horse a double handful of oats from a sack tied behind his cantle, turned the animal loose to graze, then stripped to the waist and bathed in the icy water of the creek, noting with satisfaction that the shallow wound in his arm showed no sign of infection. Afterwards he built a fire and prepared his breakfast.

As he ate his bacon and biscuits, washed down with strong black coffee, he contemplated his next move. The visit to Colbyville, while it had resulted in his meeting with the Quigleys, had given him no line on his father's whereabouts. He wouldn't trust the Quigleys, or rather the surviving Quigley, as far as he could throw an anvil, but the younger one was too dumb to be a convincing liar, so Matt believed he had been telling the truth about their presence in town having no connection with Ephraim Dixon.

Well, it just meant more of what he had been doing for over a year, riding from town to town in the hope of picking up a lead. Sooner or later, he was bound to find someone who would recognize the picture or the name, or in whom the elder Dixon had confided. Unless... Matt wouldn't let himself think of the other possibility, that his father was dead, or that he had fled east instead of west.

Breakfast over, Matt scoured his frying pan with sand from the creek, rinsed his tin cup, and poured the leftover coffee on the fire, keeping the grounds for future use. To be doubly safe, he carefully covered the ashes with dirt, after which he tightened the cinch on his saddle, and swung aboard. From his knowledge of the territory, which was now fairly extensive, he estimated that Gunnison, the nearest town of any size, would be about forty miles to the west. A good day's ride, but his mount was fresh, and he himself was hardened to the saddle. Maybe at Gunnison...

Matt had never failed to be impressed by the rugged beauty of this high country on the western slope of the Rockies. Behind him, to the east, the mountains etched a jagged line across a cloudless sky, their barren peaks above timber line dotted with patches of snow which would never melt. The narrow road he was following wound through thick stands of evergreen and aspen, and at times was paralleled by a crystal clear creek, whose tumbling waters would eventually find their way to the Pacific. Indiana had beauty, too, but of a different sort, and a feeling deep inside told him that he would never be content to return to the flatlands. Some day, when his mission was accomplished, he would find a spot in this area and put down roots.

Meanwhile, the sun reached its zenith, reminding him that he had spent too much time admiring the scenery, and still had a long way to go. He stopped briefly to rest his mount and let it drink from the stream, while he himself ate cold biscuits left over from breakfast, along with some jerky. His arm was hurting slightly, but there was still no sign of infection.

Either he had misjudged the distance to Gunnison, or he had set too slow a pace. At any rate, the sun dropped behind the western horizon when he still had some way to go. He stopped to eat his evening meal and let the horse graze, considered spending the night on the trail, but decided to push ahead. From here on it would be mostly downhill, and there was enough light from a half moon to make the road clearly visible.

At what he judged to be about ten o'clock, he was startled by the rattle of gunshots up ahead, followed by the pound of galloping hoofs. He reined up to listen, and the sounds grew louder. Soon he could tell that there was more than one rider headed his way, and then he heard men's angry voices, shouting words which he couldn't make out. The indication was that someone was being chased, and that both the pursued and the pursuers were headed his direction.

At this spot the stream was on one side, and a sheer cliff on the other, so there was no way of getting off the road. Since Matt didn't want to face a bunch of excited men, who were evidently throwing a lot of lead, he turned his horse and backtracked at a gallop.

The grade was now uphill, and Matt's horse was far from fresh. It did its best, but the sounds grew louder. Presently another horse came pounding around a bend behind him.

Its rider, more surprised than Matt, instinctively flung up an arm as though to ward off an expected bullet. The action threw his horse off stride, and the two animals bumped. Matt's lost its footing and went down, pitching him from the saddle. As he fell, he thought he saw something fly from the other man's hand. Then the fellow recovered control of his mount, and was gone.

Seconds later, while Matt lay stunned by his fall, the other riders came around the bend. The one in front, seeing Matt lying in the road, yanked his horse to a sliding stop, and yelled loudly, "Here he is, men! Hold your fire! I think he's out cold."

In this he was mistaken, for Matt, though dazed, could make out the shapes of the other riders. Then the one who had spoken, and who was apparently their leader, stepped from his saddle, bent down to lift Matt's pistol from its holster, and demanded harshly, "Can you hear me?"

"I hear you," Matt said. Now that he had been disarmed, he was hopeful that no one would shoot at him. This optimism was aided by sight of a lawman's badge worn by the one who had spoken. Matt levered himself to a sitting position, and added, "But I'm not the fellow you were chasing. While you're wasting time, he's getting away."

The lawman straightened up and motioned for silence, but with so many horses milling around, he couldn't possibly have heard the sounds made by a now distant quarry. He lost interest, anyway, when one of the men who had dismounted, called excitedly, "Here it is, Roper!" He moved up and held out a canvas bag. The man he had called Roper glanced at it, then returned his attention to Matt.

"So you're the wrong one, are you? A good try, mister, but it won't work." Before Matt realized what was happening, a pair of handcuffs were slapped on his wrists. He was yanked roughly to his feet, and a pistol jammed in his belly. His horse, which had recovered its footing and seemed uninjured, was led up beside him.

"Get in your saddle," the marshal ordered. "We'll take you back to Gunnison, and see how Judge Logan likes the sound of your wild yarn." Turning to the other men, the marshal said authoritatively, "I know how you boys feel about Old Man Yates. I liked him as much as you did. But don't try anything foolish. This killer's going to get a fair trial before we hang him."

"Wait!" Matt protested. "I don't know anything about a man named Yates. Or about that moneybag, either. Like I tried to tell you, the man you were chasing got away."

"Sure," the marshal said sarcastically. "After giving you the loot to hold for him. A likely story.

Get moving!"

Matt had never felt so helpless. It was obvious that he was presumed to have committed a robbery. Worse yet, to judge from the marshal's use of the word "killer," someone named Yates had been killed. And Matt had no alibi. Even if he could persuade someone to make the long ride to Colbyville and talk with the town marshal, it wouldn't do much good. After all, he actually *had* killed a man back there, which would be used against him, and since no one had seen him ride out, it could be claimed that he had started early enough to have reached Gunnison, done whatever the men thought he had done, and tried to make a getaway.

The citizens of Gunnison, watching the posse ride in, were plainly aroused. They shouted threats and curses at Matt as he was escorted along the main street. He was sweating profusely, and it was almost a relief when he was safely in the marshal's office, the handcuffs had been removed, and he was shoved into a cell. Almost, but not quite, for at the sound of the iron barred door clanging shut, Matt's old fear was rekindled. He wanted to hurl himself at the bars and scream.

Actually, he did neither, but sat on the edge of the cell's only bunk, and stared at the floor, not looking up until the marshal, after drawing the window curtains, presumably for fear that someone outside might shoot his prisoner, came back to look through the bars, and said with satisfaction, "I see you've got blood on your sleeve. One of our bullets must've nicked you after all."

Matt didn't bother to deny this. Even if by some

miracle they did check back with the Colbyville marshal, who could verify that the wound had been there the night before, it would have no bearing on this much more serious charge. With an effort of will, he asked, "When will I get to talk to this judge you mentioned?"

"Judge Logan? Oh, it'll be a few days. He's over at Grand Junction for his son's wedding."

"Wedding!" Matt exclaimed. "Good God, do you mean I'm going to be stuck in this jail for something I didn't do till the judge takes a notion to come back?"

"Look at it this way," the marshal said drily. "The longer Judge Logan stays away, the longer you'll be alive. Old Man Yates was a friend of his, too."

With this, the marshal turned his back on the cell, as though intending to leave. Instead, he unwisely paused to fashion a cigarette.

Matt, shaken by the marshal's certainty that he was to be hanged, and half out of his mind at the prospect of being confined to this cell for an indefinite period, reached instinctively. He lunged across the cell, reached between the bars, and yanked the marshal's sixgun out of its holster. Thumbing back the hammer, he said savagely, "Turn around real slow and unlock the door! Remember, I've got nothing to lose, not the way you tell it."

The marshal froze with his cigarette halfway to his mouth. He turned, and reached for his keys, which he had dropped in his pocket after locking the cell. His face a mask of controlled fury, he reached out and unlocked the door.

"Inside!" Matt ordered, gesturing with the pistol.

The marshal stepped stiff-legged into the cell, but the stiffness went out of him suddenly as Matt hit him behind the ear with the gunbarrel. Matt caught him before he could fall, dragged him a few feet, and laid him on the bunk. He rolled him onto his stomach, cuffed his hands behind his back, and used the marshal's belt to tie his ankles together. A piece torn from the bunk's only blanket served as a gag, and with this accomplished, Matt backed out of the cell, locked the door, and tossed the keys into a cold pot-bellied stove.

There were noises in the street to indicate that some of the crowd remained. Matt peered around the edge of the window curtain and counted half a dozen men lingering out front. All of them were armed, so he knew that it would be suicidal to open the door and try to reach his horse, which he could see at the tie rail. As a precaution, he quietly bolted the door before sitting down at the marshal's desk, prepared to wait it out. After a bit he thought of his revolver, which had been taken away from him. He found it in the top desk drawer, and exchanged it for the marshal's. At least he couldn't be accused of having stolen a gun.

Not that this made much difference. From what he had heard, there had been a robbery, in the course of which, or as an aftermath, a man by the name of Yates had been killed. He doubted that there was anyone in Gunnison who didn't believe that he, Matt Dixon, was the killer.

A small sound from the cell prompted Matt to get up and peer through the bars. The marshal's eyes were open, and he was trying to say something, twisting his feet in an effort to dislodge the gag.

Matt could imagine how uncomfortable the gag must be, and his first impulse was to loosen the knot, but he knew that he didn't dare, or the marshal would shout for help. He shook his head.

"There's no point fighting it, Marshal. Sooner or later, someone's bound to come looking for you, and he'll turn you loose. By then I intend to be a long way off."

The marshal quit struggling, and Matt added soberly, "For what it's worth, I'm not the man you were chasing. He was so surprised to see me that he lost his grip on the moneybag. Also control of his horse, which bumped mine. That's why I was lying on the road. You can believe it or not, but that's the truth."

The marshal must have heard, but he gave no indication. After a bit Matt turned away and went back to the chair. Time passed slowly, marked off by the ticking of an octagonal clock on the wall. Finally the street was quiet. Matt blew out the lamp, unbolted the door and eased it open, stood listening for a few minutes, then let himself out, closing the door quietly behind him. Every nerve on edge, he unwrapped his horse's reins from the tie rail, stepped into the saddle, and rode out of town.

An hour later, when there was still no indication of pursuit, Matt took his first deep breath. For the moment, at least, he was free. It was a wonderful feeling while it lasted. Then the euphoria wore off as he realized the gravity of his situation. In the last thirty hours or so he had killed a man. That, in itself, wasn't too serious, since he had acted in self defense. But now... now he was an escaped prisoner, guilty of assaulting an officer of the law. Worse, he was presumed to have killed yet a second man, and to have committed some kind of robbery. In short, his name would be among those listed on posters as WANTED. Which meant that he would have to change his name, which was known to the Colbyville marshal, alter his appearance, if possible, and avoid towns insofar as he could.

It was almost like... He shook his head angrily, and refused to complete the thought. There was no comparison between his situation and that of his father. Holding this in mind, he continued his flight.

Chapter Four

Three weeks had elapsed since Sheriff Ed Durham, as he was known to all the citizens of Holbrook except Ellen Troup, had been shot by the bank robber. Despite Doc Yarborough's protests, the sheriff had discarded his crutches, and was hobbling around with the aid of a cane. Fortunately, nothing had come up which couldn't be handled by the deputy, Al Gregg.

This enabled the sheriff to spend more time than usual in his office, and he was sitting there, glancing through some WANTED notices which had been dropped off by the east-bound stage, when a name jumped out and hit him like a slap in the face. Matt Dixon! Not his and Nora's Matt, surely!

It was, though. He was forced to admit this to himself as he read the details, some of which had been supplied by the Colbyville, Colorado town marshal. Age twenty-one. Yes, that would be right. A native of Indiana. Claimed to be looking for his father, name of Ephraim. Wanted now for robbery and murder committed in Gunnison. If seen, approach with caution, as he had killed twice and would not hesitate to kill again.

The sheriff, seeing his own name in print, once

again felt the fear that had dogged him for the first few years after his flight. Even worse was the thought that this criminal, a robber and murderer, was his own son. It was hard to believe, but there it was in black and white. Thank God Nora had not lived to hear about it! Especially that Matt intended to kill his own father.

The sheriff was so preoccupied with what he had just read that he didn't hear the door open. His head jerked when a man's voice asked, "Something wrong, Sheriff? You look like you'd seen a ghost."

The speaker was Hubert Nolan, who owned Slash N, the largest ranch in the region, and who was well aware of his own importance. A handsome, muscular man some five years younger than the sheriff, he was as a rule outwardly pleasant, but for some reason the sheriff had never liked him. Perhaps he was prejudiced by the fact that Nolan was more than a little interested in Ellen Troup.

The sheriff tried to erase this thought from his mind, and said mildly, "Nothing like that, Mr. Nolan. I was just day dreaming. Is there something I can do for you?"

"I'm not sure," Nolan said. "In fact on the way to town I almost changed my mind and turned back. But since I'm here. . . well, it's about Ben Gibson again."

At the mention of Gibson, Nolan had the sheriff's full attention. Gibson ran a small ranch adjacent to Nolan's Slash N, and there had been trouble between the two men before. It was a David and Goliath sort of match, and the sheriff, who liked Ben Gibson, a widower with a teen age daughter, was on his side, although he tried hard not to let this color his judgement.

"What is it this time, Mr. Nolan?"

Nolan sighed, as though he disliked what he was about to say.

"It's the same old story, Sheriff. I've been losing cattle, a few at a time, and I can't help thinking. . . damn it, I feel sorry for the man, trying to make a go of it on that two-bit ranch of his, but he's got no right stealing my cows."

"Do you have any proof that he *is*?" the sheriff asked. "If you'll think back, the last time you accused him of rustling, I rode out and went over his place without turning up a single piece of evidence. Of course if you have something definite. . ."

"No, damn it," Nolan said, looking frustrated. "Like I said, I almost kept still about it. But you've got to admit that it looks suspicious. Everyone knows Gibson has hated my guts ever since I outbid him on that little hunk of land we both wanted. He claimed he needed it so he could run a few more cattle. Maybe he did, but it was a fair deal. He just couldn't match my bid. Hell, I even offered to buy his place for more than it's worth, but he wouldn't listen to me."

The sheriff could understand why Gibson wouldn't sell. Ben and his wife Flora had built up their little ranch from nothing. Now Flora was buried on the property for which they had worked so hard. However, this had no legal significance, and the sheriff was sworn to uphold the law. He said evenly, "When you've got something I can get my teeth into, let me know. Until then, there's nothing I can do."

"No, I suppose not," Nolan acknowledged, and glanced at the sheriff's cane, which was lying on the desk. "Like I said, I almost didn't bother you. After all, crippled up like you are. . . well, when I get proof, I'll be back. But just so the ride won't be a complete waste, I'll drop over to the restaurant and have some of Ellen's good pie. Care to join me?"

"No," the sheriff said bluntly, and then, to soften the effect, "I've got some work to do right here."

Nolan shrugged, and left the office, smiling to himself. He had laid the groundwork. The next time he came to complain against Gibson, he would have some kind of proof.

Ellen's cafe was only half a block away, but rather than walk, Nolan stepped into the silver-mounted saddle of the big black which he favored, and rode to the cafe hitchrail.

For a few minutes the sheriff stared bleakly at the street. Much as he hated the thought, he couldn't blame Ellen if she married Nolan. It was the logical choice. Nolan was rich, and could give her everything she wanted. Well, almost everything. He couldn't give her love and loyalty. Nolan considered himself too important to be tied down to one woman.

The sheriff's thoughts returned to the WANTED poster, and he forgot about Nolan. Somewhere out there, the man whom he had last seen as a baby was running for his life. It was a situation the sheriff could appreciate, for he had been on the dodge himself at one time. Unlike Matt, though, he hadn't been looking for another person to kill. Somehow, the fact that he, the sheriff, was that person, didn't seem too important. That might come later.

His deputy, Al Gregg, entered the office before the sheriff could figure it out. Gregg, who had never been noted for his modesty, was even more cocksure after having held down the office alone while the sheriff was laid up, and this put an added strain on the sheriff's patience. Gregg tilted his hat to the back of his head, and said wisely, "I noticed Mr. Big Shot coming out of here. What's itching him today?"

"Nothing new," the sheriff said, not letting his impatience show. "He claims to be missing some cattle, and thinks Ben Gibson is to blame."

"Want me to go out and check?" Gregg asked quickly.

The sheriff smiled.

"Is it the cattle you're interested in, or a chance to see Ben Gibson's pretty daughter?"

Gregg was still young enough to blush, and the sheriff took him off the hook by adding, "No, there'd be no point going out there, and I don't want Ben to think we're suspicious of him. I told Nolan to come back when he had positive proof. Here's a few WANTED notices that came in on the stage. You might take a look at them, just in case."

"Sure thing," Gregg said, and held out his hand.

The sheriff had left Matt's notice on top, and he watched Al Gregg narrowly. Not that there was any reason to. The description could fit any number of men: six feet tall, brown hair and eyes, weight about one seventy, smooth-shaven.

Of course the smooth-shaven part wouldn't mean much. By now, Matt would be letting his beard grow, just as his father had twenty years ago. The sheriff still wore a beard, even though he no longer considered it necessary as a disguise.

A door banged loudly somewhere along the street, and moments later Nolan rode by, an angry expression on his face. On a hunch, the sheriff got up, took his cane, and said, "I'll be gone a few minutes. You hang around until I get back."

"Yes, sir," Gregg said, apparently prompted by something in the sheriff's tone to use the more formal form of address.

The sheriff left the office, crossed the wooden sidewalk, and headed for Ellen's restaurant, trying not to limp. He entered the door, and his first look at Ellen confirmed his guess.

"Has Nolan been giving you a bad time?"

Ellen looked grim, but she attempted to sound unconcerned.

"Nothing to get excited about," she said, shrugging. "He didn't make any ungentlemanly suggestions, if that's what you mean. I suppose, from his viewpoint, he was paying me a compliment." She met the sheriff's eyes squarely. "He asked me to marry him."

The sheriff had been expecting this for a long time, but it still came as a shock. However, he managed to say without undo emotion, "There must have been more to it than that, to make you so sore. What else did he say?"

"He said. . ." Ellen faltered, then went on with a rush, "Dern him, he said I'd be foolish to waste my life on an underpaid lawman with a gimpy leg.

That's when I told him ~~to go to hell.~~"

The sheriff's relief was so great that he couldn't help laughing. It was the first time he had heard Ellen swear. He could imagine the effect it must have had on Nolan, who was used to getting his own way.

After a bit, Ellen joined in the laughter. When she was able to talk, she said wryly, "It's a good thing there aren't any customers. They'd think we were crazy."

"They'd be halfway right," the sheriff said, sobering. "Nolan isn't a good man to have as an enemy. But let's worry about that later. There's something else I want to tell you, something that's just come up. Could you lock the door so we won't be interrupted?"

Ellen nodded, locked the door, and sat down on one of the stools at the counter. The sheriff took an adjacent stool, looked at her thoughtfully for a moment, then said without preface, "My son Matt is wanted for murder and robbery. I just got a notice in today's mail."

"Oh, no!" Ellen gasped. "Are you sure?"

"I'm sure," the sheriff said. "They even had his name, and everything else fits. But I still can't believe it."

Ellen frowned.

"I thought you said. . . "

"Oh, I'm satisfied it's Matt they're looking for. What I mean is that I can't believe he'd do what they claim. Not after having been raised by Nora. And aside from that, if he was as bad as they make out, why would he be using his *right* name? It doesn't make sense."

"Lots of things don't," Ellen said. "So try not to get your hopes up. After all, it's been years and years since you saw him. Almost anything could have happened. Of course I hope you're right, and that it's all a mistake. Thank goodness there's not one chance in a thousand that you'll get involved."

"I already am," the sheriff said. "You haven't heard all of it yet. According to the notice, he told several people that he was looking for his father, Ephraim Dixon." He hesitated, then added grimly, "He intends to kill me."

Ellen's breath caught in her throat, and she impulsively reached out to lay a hand on the sheriff's arm. Neither of them could think of anything to say, and after a bit the sheriff rose, limped to the door, and went out onto the street.

Watching him, Ellen began to cry, something she seldom did.

Chapter Five

As the sheriff had surmised, Matt had quit shaving. Now, after almost a month of keeping to the back country and living off the land, in which game was plentiful, his reflection in a still pool looked unfamiliar to him, and he decided that it would be safe to visit a town and replenish his supplies. He had been travelling in a generally south-westerly direction, and believed that he would now be in Arizona. There was some comfort in the thought that leaving Colorado might reduce his chances of being caught. At any rate it was a risk he had to take, since he was out of salt and flour, and running low on ammunition for his saddle gun.

The place at which he made his re-entry into civilization was little more than a trading post, although it bore the imposing name of *El Pueblo Grande*. In addition to a saloon, which was the one essential ingredient of every town in the west, there were a dozen houses, most of them adobe, and a general store. Several blanketed Indians were hunkered down in the shade of the store's wooden awning. Their eyes followed him as he pulled up at the hitch rail and dismounted. Since he still had the typical mid-westerner's mistrust of Indians, he took his carbine and saddlebags with him into the store.

The proprietor, a scrawny, white-haired man with leathery skin, took note of this, and said good naturedly, "Don't worry about them Injuns out front. They're from a reservation over near the canyon, and too lazy to steal. Besides which, they know they'd get caught, and thrown into the reservation hoosegow. What can I do for you?"

"I need half a pound of salt and some flour," Matt said. He supposed the man had been referring to the Grand Canyone of the Colorado, which he had gazed at in awe the day before. "Also some shells for this carbine. I suppose you carry ammunition?"

"Carry 'most everything from axes to corsets," the man said. "And that's no joke. The corsets, I mean. Nobody around here would wear one, but the Injuns use the stays to make their traps." He went behind the counter, and added, "You just passin' through, or do you aim to stay a while?"

"Passing through," Matt told him, vastly relieved that the man had shown no more than normal curiosity. He glanced around at the store, which seemed unusually well stocked for such an out-of-the-way place. "You must do a good business here, from the looks of your shelves. Are there many ranches nearby?"

"Nope," the merchant said, shaking his head. "Most of my stuff goes to the Injuns. The local agent. . . say, you wouldn't be a government man, would you?"

Matt assured him that he wasn't, but the storekeeper didn't finish his sentence. Probably, Matt supposed, he and the Indian agent had some kind of slightly illegal arrangement. Well, that was none of his business. To change the subject, he asked, "Do you get many travellers through here?"

"Funny you'd ask that," the man said. "As a rule, I'll go a month at a time without seeing a stranger. Now I've had two in one day, you and a bounty hunter that came by this morning."

"Bounty hunter?" Matt said, tensing. "How could you tell? Did he say so?"

"Didn't have to. I can spot one a mile away. He didn't deny it, though, when I asked him. Claimed to be lookin' for some female. Not that it's necessarily true. Bounty hunters are almost as bad as Injuns when it comes to lying."

Relieved, Matt breathed more easily. By then the storekeeper had put a box of cartridges alongside the other supplies.

"Anything else, mister? I've got some right good whiskey in the back room. Not," he added quickly, "that I'd ever sell any to the Injuns."

"No, thanks," Matt said, paying for his purchases and pocketing the change. Apparently the old man still wasn't sure that Matt wasn't a government agent, but that, too, was none of Matt's concern. "I'll be getting along. I want to put a few more miles behind me before night. So long."

"Adios," the man said, and added, "If you're headed south, you may catch up with that bounty hunter. That's the way he was going."

"Me, too," Matt said. "I hope I meet up with him. I'd like to hear what that female did that would put a price on her head."

There was no answer, so Matt left the store. The Indians were just as he had seen them before, and he felt a little guilty for having suspected that they would steal from him. He was sorry for them, penned up on a reservation when they were by nature nomads.

In case the storekeeper should be watching, Matt actually did ride south from the trading post, but he had no intention of catching up with the bounty hunter. Maybe the man really was looking for a woman, but he could also know about the trouble at Gunnison. Matt didn't doubt that there was a reward out for him.

Five miles out of town, another road angled off to the southeast. A weather-beaten sign bore the wording, "Holbrook—50 miles." Matt got down to examine the ground, couldn't find any fresh tracks leading that way, so left the main road and headed in the direction indicated by the sign. He had no particular reason for going to Holbrook, but he didn't want to follow the bounty hunter, and he couldn't go west without being blocked by the canyon.

The country through which Matt was now riding was quite different from what he was used to. Instead of thick forests, there were now only scattered dwarf cedars and clumps of desert vegetation. The soft matting of needles had given away to gravelly soil, with an occasional good sized boulder. When Matt stopped at noon to rest his horse, he checked its hoofs for pebbles which might have been picked up, and which could cause trouble. There were none of these, but he discovered that the horse's shoes were wearing thin, and that the one on the left front hoof was loose. By the time he made camp for the night, still some twenty miles short of Holbrook, the shoe was so loose that he had to take it off, using pliers from his saddlebag to pull the nails.

The spot he had chosen was alongside a small stream, which provided water for his horse, as well as for the coffeepot. Darkness came quickly and, soon after eating, Matt lay down beside the dying fire, using his saddle as a pillow. He didn't fall asleep immediately, but lay looking up at the stars, and reviewing his situation. For the last three weeks and more he had been so intent on avoiding capture that he hadn't given much thought to his primary purpose, which was to find his father and avenge the injustice done his mother. Now that he had changed his appearance, and had successfully avoided capture, he could pick up where he had left off. Not as Matt Dixon, though. He would have to assume a new identity.

After considerable thought, he settled on the name Martin Davis. It had no special significance, but was ordinary sounding, and easy to remember. He wondered what name had been substituted for Ephraim Dixon. Surely something, or his father would have been picked up by some lawman years ago, and returned to Indiana.

Despite himself, Matt couldn't help comparing his own situation with his father's. Each of them had taken flight to avoid jail. Probably they had both changed their names, as well as their appearances. Had his father grown a beard and mustache? The old daguerrotype depicted him as smooth shaven, which might be why no one had recognized it.

Matt stirred impatiently. Except on the surface, there was no similarity between the two cases. He, Matt—or should he start thinking of himself as Martin?—had commited no crime. Well, not unless you counted knocking out a town marshal and breaking jail, which had been justified. He hadn't deserted a wife and child. His father had, and by God he was going to pay for it!

After a restless night, Matt arose, bathed, and cooked his breakfast. His horse, which he had left on picket, hadn't found much to eat in this relatively barren area, so Matt gave it an extra ration of oats. He noticed that the animal favored the hoof from which he had removed the shoe. Apparently some damage had been done before he had discovered that it was loose. With something akin to dismay, he realized that he wouldn't be able to ride until the horse had been re-shod, and the leg was well. Back in Indiana he would have thought nothing of a day-long walk, but during the last year he had acquired the typical cowboy's dislike of going more than a dozen yards on foot. In addition, he was now wearing high heeled boots which were not designed for walking.

In any case, one decision had been made for him. He would have to go to Holbrook, like it or not, where there would undoubtedly be a blacksmith shop. Leading the horse, he started out.

It was dark when he reached Holbrook, and by then both he and the horse were limping. Holbrook, while considerably larger than some of the towns through which he had passed on his travels, wasn't big enough to make finding the blacksmith shop difficult. There was nobody on duty, and the forge was cold, which could be expected at this time of night. However, the smithy was attached to a livery barn, and when Matt entered the latter, a door opened, and a man came out of what were apparently his living quarters.

The liveryman was short, and even in the dim light from the open doorway, Matt could see that he had a peg leg. When he spoke, his voice was rusty, and sounded irritable.

"Well, speak up, mister. What do you want?"

"A place to stable my horse," Matt said, his own voice a little harsh after the long tiresome walk. "And in the morning, I want him re-shod. Are you the blacksmith?"

"No," the man said shortly. "That'd be Moose Dreyfuss. I'm Abner Boggs. The stall will be a dollar for the night, cash in advance."

"Including hay and oats?" Matt asked, and when the man grunted what was apparently supposed to mean yes, Matt took out a silver dollar and handed it over. This seemed to improve the peg-leg's disposition, so Matt guessed that he could have talked him into a lower price. Boggs pointed at an empty stall, and went back into the living quarters, from which he re-emerged with a lighted lantern which he hung from a wire hook fastened to a rafter.

"Moose gets here at six o'clock in the morning, but it takes him half an hour to get the forge hot. By the way, have you got a name?"

Matt caught himself in time, and said, "Davis, Martin Davis." He led his horse into the stall, removed its bridle and saddle, and used the saddle blanket to rub it down. Since he didn't have much confidence in the liveryman, he forked hay into the manger, checked to make sure the waterpail was full, and located an oat bin, from which he transferred a scoopful to the feed box. With his saddlebags over his left arm, and carrying the carbine in his left hand, he left the barn. After so many nights on the trail, he felt justified in treating himself to a real bed, and he had noticed a hotel sign as he rode in.

First, though, he wanted a drink. There was a saloon in the block, identified by lamplight spilling out over its half-doors. Matt went in, and at once wished that he hadn't, for it was immediately apparent that he had walked in on a ticklish situation.

Four or five patrons had backed away from the bar and were staring nervously at three others, two of them rough looking individuals with low slung holsters, the third much younger, and wearing a star on which Matt could read the word "Deputy."

Either through his own carelessness, or due to the contrivance of the two hard cases, the one with the badge was between them, which would put him in an untenable position if trouble broke out.

Matt had no idea what was brewing, nor did he want any part of other people's troubles. He had enough of his own. Before he could back through the batwings, however, the hard case who was face to face with the deputy made a quick draw. At the same time, his partner, most likely acting on a prearranged signal, drew his own pistol and aimed it at the deputy's back.

Matt, without stopping to think, whipped his pistol out of the holster, yelled, "Over here!" and then shot the second man before he could pull the trigger. The fellow was knocked backward by the bullet, made a futile attempt to grab onto the bar, and went down, his head banging on the brass rail. The other tough-looking character, whose gun had spoken almost simultaneously with Matt's, swivelled his head, found himself looking into the muzzle of Matt's gun, and very wisely obeyed Matt's command to drop his own.

There were footsteps in the street, the batwings parted, and a man wearing a star marked "Sheriff" came into the room, a pistol in his right hand, the other hand gripping a cane. He took in the situation at a glance, and swung his gun muzzle toward Matt, who still had his revolver trained on the man at the bar. Matt slowly lowered his gun and slid it into its holster. Without otherwise moving, he said evenly, "Don't jump to the wrong conclusion, Sheriff. It wasn't me that shot your deputy. I've got plenty of witnesses to prove it."

The sheriff glanced at the customers, and one of them, apparently their self-appointed spokesman, said clearly, "That's right, Sheriff. He walked in on the middle of things. That mean looking fellow by the bar shot Al Gregg. Killed him, I reckon."

Evidently satisfied with this verification, the sheriff swung his gun away from Matt and crossed to the bar. Keeping his eyes on the hard case, he kicked the dropped gun across the room.

"Put your hands behind your back, and don't try anything cute. I'm just itching to put a bullet through you."

The man complied, and the sheriff shifted his weight to his good leg so that he could use his left hand to snap cuffs on the man's wrists. He had to drop his cane to do this, and when he stooped to recover it, he felt the deputy's wrist, although this hardly seemed necessary, since there was a bullet hole directly over the young man's heart. The sheriff recovered his cane, stood up, and faced the killer.

"Dewey, hanging's too good for you, but that's what you'll get. You likely know where the jail is. Start moving!"

The killer headed for the door, with the sheriff behind him. Just before leaving, the sheriff said to Matt, "Sorry I threw down on you, boy. What's your name?"

"Martin Davis." This time it came without any hesitation.

"I'm Ed Durham," the sheriff said. "I'd appreciate it if you'd drop over to my office when you've got time. This business is pretty cut-and-dried, but I still have to make a report."

"Sure," Matt said. "Just as soon as I wash the dust out of my throat."

"I'm obliged," the sheriff said, and, turning his head slightly, "One of you fellows get Doc Yarborough. Tell him to take care of my deputy. I don't care what happens to the other one."

Outside, herding his prisoner across the street to the jail, the sheriff, although he was alert for an escape attempt, wasn't thinking too much about the man in front of him. His thoughts were on the young stranger who called himself Martin Davis, but who he was sure was his son, Matt. All right, so he hadn't seen him since he was a baby, and now he was grown and wearing a beard. But he couldn't change his eyes, which were a dead giveaway. They were Nora's eyes.

Chapter Six

While Matt finished his drink, the customer who had left returned with another man whom the bartender addressed as "Doc." The doctor, after a quick glance at Matt, knelt down and verified that both the deputy and the would-be backshooter were dead. By this time a number of townsmen had come into the saloon, presumably attracted by the gunshots. The doctor directed four of them to take the bodies over to his office, and when they had left, moved up beside Matt and held out his hand.

"I'm the local sawbones, as you may have guessed. Name's Yarborough."

"Martin Davis," Matt said, shaking the doctor's hand. "Glad to meet you, although I can think of more pleasant circumstances. Not that I know exactly what the circumstances *are*. Nobody had told me what started the trouble."

"According to Ned Wiley. . . he's the man who came for me. . . it shouldn't have happened at all. It seems that the deputy, Al Gregg, started asking the two strangers some personal questions. Things like what their names were, and where they were from. Could be he had visions of nabbing somebody wanted by the law. He's been feeling his oats ever since he held down Sheriff Durham's office a couple of weeks while the sheriff was laid up. The sheriff would have handled it differently, and probably could have gotten away with it, but Gregg, lacking the know-how that comes from experience, was out of his depth. It's too bad. Al Gregg was a nice enough lad." The doctor shook his head, and added philosophically, "Well, it's a little late to do anything about it now. Will you be staying with us a while?"

"Just until my horse is back in shape," Matt said. "He came up lame today. I'll know more about it in the morning. I'll be around until he's fit to travel. Well, the sheriff asked me to drop by his office, so I'd better not keep him waiting. Been nice meeting you."

"Thanks," the doctor said. "You'll like the sheriff. For that matter, there are worse towns than Holbrook. We don't have trouble like this very often."

Matt paid for his drink and left the saloon. Crossing the street, he wondered if saloons were bad luck for him. Twice now he had gone into one simply for a drink, and twice he had killed a man, both of them men he had never seen before. Well, maybe that wasn't strictly true; he might have seen the Quigleys, but if so, he had been too young to remember them.

The sheriff's office was typical of others he had seen, a small, narrow building with a desk and two chairs in front, and a cell, or, in this case, two cells, at the rear. The sheriff, seated at the desk, gestured toward one of the other chairs, and said politely, "Have a seat, Mr. Davis. Sorry to have to bother you this way."

"No bother," Matt said. "I've got nothing to do anyhow, except find a place to spend the night. I don't suppose that'll be much of a problem, since I noticed a hotel down the street."

"The Antlers," the sheriff volunteered. "No, you'll have no trouble getting a room there. The hotel hasn't been filled since Jase Ettinger built it, some nine years ago. You'd be welcome to sleep here, but I don't imagine you'd care for your neighbor." He gestured toward the back of the room, and Matt could see the glow of a cigarette. He looked back at the sheriff, and found him studying Matt thoughtfully.

Matt's heart skipped a beat. Had the sheriff recognized him, perhaps from his description on a WANTED dodger?

If so, the sheriff gave no indication, but said mildly, "Actually, I guess there's not much I need to ask you. The men who were in the saloon agree that all you did was prevent my deputy from being shot in the back. It's just too bad that the gunslinger back there in the cell couldn't have been killed, too. It would save the county a lot of trouble and expense. I don't suppose you've ever run into the pair before?"

Matt shook his head.

"They were strangers to me, Sheriff."

"I figured as much. However, I think I know who they are, or were. The bugger back there won't talk, but he fits the description of a fellow who's wanted for bank robbery in New Mexico. Not that he'll be going back there to face the charge. He'll be hanged for murder right here in

Holbrook as soon as Judge Jensen holds the trial. By the way, do you expect to be around for it? It'll probably be in a day or two."

"No," Matt said, then changed it to, "I can't say for sure. I've got a lame horse, and won't be able to leave until he's all right."

"Well, if there's anything I can do for you while you're here, let me know." He frowned. "I don't suppose. . ."

"Suppose what, Sheriff?"

"Nothing, probably. I was about to say that I'm going to need a new deputy, but you no doubt have something better to do. What you saw tonight wouldn't make the job look very attractive."

"No," Matt agreed. "It wouldn't. Good night."

Walking to the hotel, Matt thought about the sheriff's surprising offer of a job. Of course he wouldn't accept it. Or would he? Maybe it would be better than keeping on the run until the trouble back in Gunnison blew over. After all, who would expect a man on the dodge to be wearing a star? The sheriff seemed like a decent sort of man to work for. And Matt's pocket money was at a low ebb. He had some savings in a bank back in Indiana, but under the present circumstances he couldn't safely send for it. Maybe if he took the job for a month or two. . .

After Matt had left his office, the sheriff sat for a long time in deep thought. The first shock of seeing his son after so many years had begun to wear off, and he debated what he should do. The natural move, of course, would be to lock Matt, or whatever he chose to call himself, in the empty cell, and send word to the town marshal of Gunnison to come and get him, but every fibre of his being rebelled at the idea. He had abandoned Matt once; he wasn't going to betray him now, even though Matt had admitted to the Colbyville town marshal that he was looking for his father in order to kill him.

The sheriff's reverie was interrupted by his prisoner calling from the cell, "Hey! Ain't you going to give me anything to eat?"

This brought the sheriff out of his chair. He picked up the lamp in his left hand, foregoing use of the cane, and limped back to stare contemptuously at the prisoner. Suspecting a trick, he was careful to remain more than an arm's length from the cell.

"You'll get breakfast in the morning. If you haven't eaten supper it's your own tough luck. Have you decided to tell me your name?"

"Go to hell!" the man snarled, and the sheriff shrugged and turned away. He wasn't worried about the prisoner's escaping, for the jail was well built, and had withstood attempted jailbreaks in the past. Presumably the man would get no outside help, surely none from any of Holbrook's citizens. Just to be safe, though, the sheriff pocketed the key before leaving the office, and locked the front door after him as an extra precaution.

Holbrook's main street was quiet now. Even the saloon was dark, for it stayed open late only on Saturday nights. Ordinarily, most of the townsfolk would be asleep by this time. Tonight, on account of the killing, they were probably awake, talking about what had happened, and looking forward to the trial, which would be a break in the monotony. Some of them might even be feeling sad because of what had happened to Al Gregg. The sheriff wondered if Laura Gibson, Ben's eighteen year old daughter, would shed a tear when she found out about it. He thought she would, for she was a warm-hearted girl, but he doubted that she would suffer too much. She and Al Gregg had gone to the Saturday night dances together, but they had not been sweethearts.

While these thoughts were running through his head, the sheriff had been making his nightly patrol, a little slower than usual because of his bad leg. He found the front door of the mercantile unlocked, with the padlock in place through the hasp, but not pushed shut. It was the second time this had happened in the last month. He'd have to speak to Lew Gordy about it in the morning. However, since no one inside the store could have left the padlock in that position, he merely snapped it shut, checked the back of the building to make sure the rear door was secure, and continued his rounds.

As usual, he looked across at the restaurant. Ellen's bedroom curtains were drawn, but enough light showed through to indicate that she was still up.

This time he had to knock. After a bit, the door between cafe and bedroom was opened, and Ellen came into sight. She had apparently been ready to go to bed, but had stopped to put on a wrapper over her night gown. There was enough light from her bedroom for her to recognize the sheriff, and she unbolted the door.

"Come in, Ed. I wasn't really expecting you, after what happened at the saloon."

"So you know."

"Of course." She laughed softly. "Haven't you lived in Holbrook long enough to realize that you can't sneeze without the whole town hearing about it?"

She bolted the door, and the sheriff followed her back into the bedroom. They embraced briefly before she put her hands against him and gently pushed him away.

"Your heart isn't in it. What's wrong? Are you feeling bad on account of Al Gregg? I shouldn't have asked that. Of course you are. We all are, but at least you can't blame yourself. From what I've been told, he brought it on himself. Isn't that right?"

"Yes," the sheriff said. "But there's something you don't know. A stranger walked into the saloon in the middle of things. He killed one of the. . . "

"I've heard about that, too," Ellen cut in, looking puzzled. "But I don't see what difference it makes."

"Even though the stranger was my own son Matt?"

Ellen's eyes widened, and for a long moment she was speechless. Then she said almost in a whisper, "Are you sure? I was told that his name was Davis."

"And folks think mine is Durham," the sheriff said. "A man on the run isn't likely to go around using his right name. I ought to know."

"Did he. . . did you. . . "

"No, he didn't tell me his right name, and I

didn't let on I knew who he was. But I'm sure, as sure as I am that we're standing here. When he was born, everybody said he had his mother's eyes. He still has, of course, and he looks like her in other respects. Besides which he fits the description on the notice, except that he now has a beard. It's Matt, all right. God, why did he have to come here, of all places?"

"Probably some people would call it fate," Ellen said, and added quickly, "Do you suppose he recognized you, too, and just kept still about it?"

"No. All he'd have to go on would be somebody's description, and maybe an old daguerrotype I once had taken. But it's been close to twenty years, and in the picture I didn't have a beard. Besides, if he'd recognized me, I would have known. I've been studying faces for a long time, figuring out who was lying and who was telling the truth. I would have known."

"You're right, of course," Ellen said. She sat down on the edge of the bed, and gestured toward the chair. "Where is he now?"

"At the hotel," the sheriff said, and sat down wearily in the chair, laying his cane across his knees. "His horse went lame on him, and he can't leave town until it's fit to travel. Damn it, I wish he'd steal a horse and ride out during the night. No, I take that back. I don't think he's a horse thief any more than I think he did what they accuse him of in Gunnison." He looked at Ellen, and smiled ruefully. "Would you believe it? I offered him Al Gregg's job. I must be crazy."

"No," Ellen said. "You're not crazy. You're just in an impossible situation. Probably one nobody's ever faced before. Why, even if you were to decide to turn him in, it would likely come out that you're his father. When word got back to Indiana. . ."

"I'm not worried about that," the sheriff said, and he was a little surprised to realize that he really meant it. "If it would get Matt out of trouble, I'd do anything."

Ellen didn't comment, and after a bit the sheriff raised his eyes and found her looking at him, her expression unreadable. They were silent for what seemed like a long time, then he said, "No, that isn't true. I couldn't do anything that would mean losing you. If I had you to lose, that is. I know I didn't have much to offer even before this last problem came up. You could do a lot better. Maybe if I left. . ."

Surprisingly, Ellen smiled.

"Do you know what I think, Ed? I think you need a good night's sleep. You're beginning to talk as if you really *were* crazy. We'll talk about this tomorrow. Okay?"

"Okay," the sheriff said, and rose to his feet. This time he kissed her as though he meant it, and his ardor was matched by hers, but she eased him away.

"Go get your sleep, Sheriff. Everything else can wait. Come on, I'll let you out."

Chapter Seven

Matt, still carrying his carbine and saddlebags, entered the Antlers Hotel to find the lobby deserted, although an oil lamp on a wall bracket was still burning, and provided some slight illumination. The lobby itself was only about fifteen feet square, with a half dozen chairs scattered about, a small counter, behind which several keys dangled from nails driven into the wall, and a flimsy looking iron safe. The floor was uncarpeted, so Matt's boots made considerable noise as he crossed toward the counter. Enough noise, at any rate, to bring the proprietor into sight from an adjoining room.

At least Matt assumed him to be the proprietor, and this assumption was borne out when the newcomer, a fat man with only a halo of white hair around an otherwise bald head, moved up behind the counter, looked at Matt with more than passing interest, and said, "You must be the gentleman who got mixed up in that fracas over at the saloon. I'm Jake Ettinger. Are you looking for a place to stay?"

Matt nodded.

"It'll probably be just for tonight, though. That

is if my horse is in good shape tomorrow. I'll know for sure after the blacksmith looks him over."

"In any case, you're welcome," Ettinger said. "Rooms are a dollar a night. Cheaper by the week or month if you decide to stay that long." He rubbed a fat hand over his bald head, and added rather hesitantly, "If it was me, I'd likely want to hang around for the trial. I mean being as you're really the one who caught the killer and plugged his partner."

"Oh, I guess he would have been caught anyway. The sheriff got there in a hurry, especially for a man with a limp. Has he been that way long?"

"Sheriff Durham? No, only a month or so. He got shot in the leg stopping a bank robbery." The hotelman frowned, as though struck by a new idea. "When he had Al Gregg helping him, it wasn't so bad, but now. . . well, this town would be in a peck of trouble if something came up and all we had to protect us was a sheriff with a gimpy leg."

Matt didn't like the hotelman's choice of words, or his tone of voice. You'd think that inasmuch as the sheriff had acquired his limp protecting the bank where Ettinger probably kept his money, the fellow would be a little more appreciative. Matt was tempted to point this out, but restrained himself, and said merely, "I'd prefer a room facing the street, if possible. Here's my dollar."

"Yes, sir," Ettinger said, apparently sensing Matt's adverse reaction, and possibly wishing he hadn't spoken so bluntly. "There's two rooms on the front, but one of them I save for the whiskey drummer. Here's a key to the other one."

Matt took the key, and climbed the unrailed stairs to the upper floor, where another lamp provided enough light so that he could see the numbers on the doors. He approached the one which matched his key, unlocked it, and went in, dropping his saddlebags on the floor. Still holding the carbine, he struck a match and lit a lamp which was on a rickety chest of drawers.

The room was small, and the bed lumpy, but this came as no surprise. He had spent quite a few nights in other hotel rooms which might have been poured into the same mold. After locking the door, he stood his carbine in a corner, then crossed over to the room's only window, which, as had been promised, overlooked the street. The air was stuffy, so he raised the bottom sash, propping it up with a stick which had been left there for that purpose. As he did, he noticed movement on the opposite side of the street. There was enough moonlight for him to make out the form of a man, whom he recognized from his limp as being the sheriff. Out of curiosity, he continued to watch while the sheriff went from store to store, testing the doors to make sure they were locked. Finally one of the doors was opened to him and he went in.

Matt didn't bother to draw the curtain, but backed away from the window, and, after hanging his holstered gun on a bedpost, took off his outer clothing. He shouldn't be visible from outside, but even if he were, it didn't matter. He hardly thought that watching a man get ready for bed would be enough of a novelty to merit anyone's attention. He took one last look around the room, then blew out the lamp.

As he had expected, the mattress was lumpy, but it wasn't this which kept him from falling asleep. Nor was it merely the recollection of having killed a man, although this, in itself, was disturbing. What really kept him awake was thinking about the sheriff. Here was a man who had been wounded in the line of duty, but was continuing to do his job, even though walking on his bad leg must be painful. Yet if the proprietor's attitude were any criterion, folks would conveniently forget the circumstances, and categorize him as—how had the hotelman expressed it?—just a "sheriff with a gimpy leg."

Not, Matt reminded himself, that it was any concern of his. it, he had taken an immediate liking to the man. Maybe he *would* accept that offer of a deputy's job, if the sheriff was serious about it. At least until the sheriff was fit again, or found someone else to take over.

Having decided this, Matt fell asleep.

The sheriff, too, lay awake longer than usual. After leaving the cafe, he had stopped at his office to make sure that his prisoner was secure, then gone to the two-room house which he rented from Rex Bates, the banker. It was little more than a shack, but it satisfied the sheriff's needs. About all he used it for was a place to sleep, as he ate his meals at the restaurant, and spent the rest of the time either in his office or going about his official duties. Except for the week when he had been forced to stay in bed just after having had his leg broken, during which time Ellen had brought him his food.

Tonight his leg was hurting more than usual,

probably, he supposed, because of his having made the rounds of the business block, a chore which had been taken over by Al Gregg since the night of the attempted bank robbery. The pain was enough to keep him awake, but even after it subsided, he couldn't sleep. The knowledge that his son was a wanted criminal had disturbed him deeply, and this, added to the shock of actually seeing him and talking with him, made sleep elusive.

It was strange, the way a man's past finally caught up with him. All these years he had been hating himself for having deserted Nora and Matt, but he had tried to salve his conscience with the thought that Nora had probably gotten a divorce and remarried. She would certainly have had plenty of opportunities, for she had rejected many suitors before accepting his proposal.

Constantly on the move as he had been for several years, and using the assumed name of Ed Durham, there had been no way for him to know what was going on in Indiana. Until about three years ago, that was, when a man from back there whom he had known only by sight, had stopped overnight in Holbrook on his way to California. The fellow hadn't recognized Holbrook's sheriff with his changed appearance and different name, but like most folks, he had been only too willing to talk about "back home." Over a glass of whiskey with the sheriff in the saloon, he had mentioned that long-ago shooting, and, after a little adroit questioning, had revealed that the deserted wife had lost her farm, and had never remarried.

More recently, the sheriff had heard of Nora's death, but none of this had prepared him for seeing

Matt in person, or finding out that Matt had vowed to kill him.

What should he do? Reveal his true identity to Matt? No, that wouldn't solve anything. Matt would probably try to carry out his threat. And possibly succeed, for the sheriff, although he was confident of his ability to defend himself, couldn't shoot his own son.

Or should he, without revealing who he was, arrest Matt and send word to the town marshal of Gunnison? He could pretend that he had recognized Matt from his description on the WANTED notice.

Probably he could get away with it, but once again he rejected the idea. Not only was Matt his son, he might be innocent of the crimes with which he was charged. Now that the sheriff had actually met and talked with him, he found it even harder to believe that Matt would be a robber or murderer.

It was long past midnight when the sheriff fell asleep, still having found no satisfactory solution to his dilema. He awoke, unrested, at first light, and forced himself to get up. As he washed, he noticed his reflection in the cracked mirror above the basin. The face staring back at him was that of an old man. Well, he told himself wryly, he certainly wouldn't be recognizable as the young, smooth-shaven man in the daguerrotype. Every cloud had its silver lining, or so they said.

Using his cane, he went to the cafe, where he found the door unlocked. Ellen was not in sight, but he could hear her moving about in the kitchen, from which came the savory odor of frying bacon. Then she called cheerfully, "I'll be out in a minute,

Ed. I suppose you want the usual?"

"Same as always," he called back, a little puzzled at how she had been so sure who it was that had come in. Then it dawned on him. That blasted cane! She had heard it tapping on the bare floor. ~~Doggone it~~, he was going to get rid of it, doctor or no doctor. It was almost as bad as being peg-legged, like old Abner Boggs at the livery stable.

Ellen came in from the kitchen, looking even prettier than usual with her face flushed from the heat of the stove. She was carrying a plate of food which she placed on the counter. Smiling, she said lightly, "You look like ~~death~~ warmed over, Ed. Maybe this breakfast will bring you back to life."

"Maybe," the sheriff said. He hadn't been hungry, but at sight of hot cakes, fried eggs, and bacon, his appetite returned, and by the time Ellen brought him a cup of steaming coffee, he had made inroads into the food.

Ellen grinned, and said with relief, "I guess you're not ready for the undertaker after all. Shall I bring some more flapjacks?"

Before the sheriff could answer, the door opened and Matt came into the cafe. He nodded to the sheriff, then looked appreciatively at Ellen.

"Are you open for business, Ma'am?"

"It's 'miss,' not 'ma'am,' " Ellen said. "And yes, the place is open. Have a stool, unless you'd prefer eating at a table. Do you know Sheriff Durham?"

"Yes'm," Matt said.

Before he could add anything, the sheriff said, "This is Martin Davis, the man I told you about last night. Davis, meet Ellen Troup."

"A pleasure," Matt said, nodding at Ellen. "I'll sit at the counter, thanks." He glanced at the sheriff's plate, and added, "What the sheriff has looks fine to me, except I'd prefer the eggs scrambled if it isn't too much trouble. I've got a constitutional objection to egg whites, unless they're mixed up so I can't recognize them."

"Scrambled they'll be," Ellen said, and went back into the kitchen.

Matt took the second stool from the sheriff, so as not to crowd him, and remained silent as the sheriff ate. Some folks didn't like mixing conversation with their meals, and the sheriff might be one of them. Matt took a casual look around the room, noting that everything was neat and clean. This Miss Troup must be efficient as well as good looking. Good looking for an older woman, that is. He guessed she must be in her thirties, which to him put her in that group. He remembered seeing the sheriff go into one of the store buildings last night, and realized that this was the one. Well, even a sheriff was entitled to other interests than just catching criminals or locking up drunks. He admired the man's taste.

The sheriff had almost cleaned his plate before Ellen brought Matt's breakfast, but apparently he felt as Matt did about interrupting another person's meal with talk. However, he didn't leave, but made himself a cigarette and lit it. By this time two other customers had come in, both of whom Matt remembered having seen in the saloon the night before. They spoke with respect to the sheriff, and looked at Matt speculatively. Wondering, he supposed, if he made it a habit to go around shooting people. He caught the sheriff studying him, too, but didn't think much about it. After all, he was an unknown quantity. He wondered how they would react if they were told that he was wanted by the law for supposed murder and robbery.

The sheriff broke the silence by saying, "Miss Troup has weekly rates, in case you decide to stay around a while." Without waiting for a reply, he got up, took his cane, and left the cafe.

Matt finished his coffee, paid for the meal and, after complimenting Ellen on the quality of the food, also left. He hesitated only briefly before crossing to the sheriff's office. Might as well let the sheriff know his decision.

To his surprise, the office was empty, as was the cell in which the hard-case had been confined. Before Matt could become alarmed, they both came in, the prisoner in front, the sheriff two steps behind him, with his hand resting on his holstered pistol.

"Took him out back to the privy," he explained. "I'll be with you as soon as I lock him up."

Matt didn't say anything, but watched with interest as the sheriff returned his prisoner to his cell and locked the door. When the sheriff returned to the front of the room, Matt said, "If you still want me as a deputy, I'll take the job."

There was an almost imperceptible hesitation before the sheriff said heartily, "Good. I can use you, all right. Of course, the pay isn't much, only forty a month."

"That's all right," Matt said. "But there's one thing I want to make clear. I'm not taking the job permanently, just until you find somebody else to replace me."

"That's understood," the sheriff said. "I'll swear you in and give you a badge, but first I've got to go back to the cafe and get our prisoner some breakfast. Otherwise he'll start ~~~~~~~~. You're not in a big hurry, are you?"

"No," Matt said. "But if you don't mind a suggestion, why not swear me in first, and let me get the grub? If I'm going to work for you, I might as well get started."

"Fair enough," the sheriff said. "Hold up your right hand."

Afterward, going to the restaurant, Matt wondered if he had made the right decision. Well, right or wrong, he would stick with it. He just hoped he wouldn't have reason to regret it.

Chapter Eight

While Matt was talking with the sheriff, another conversation was in progress some nine miles south of Holbrook, between Nolan, owner of Slash N, and Dakota Groves. The latter, a hatchet-faced man of about thirty, with his right ear lobe missing as the result of a saloon brawl, was ostensibly just one of the Slash N cowpokes, but he had been hired more for his dexterity with a sixgun than for his ability to handle a rope. His primary function was to make sure that Nolan stayed alive—not a small task in view of the number of enemies the rancher had made.

It has been said that in order to get to the top it is necessary to step on a few toes, and if this is true, Nolan had far exceeded his quota. A goodly portion of his domain was made up of what had formerly been small outfits, each of which had been operated by an owner, with the help of his wife, and possibly one or two hired riders. Over the last ten years Nolan had acquired these properties, most of them by making life so intolerable that the owners had pulled stakes and gone elsewhere. Two especially stubborn individuals had met with "accidents," and one, thanks to a weak moment on

Nolan's part, which he himself still couldn't understand, had been bought out legitimately.

By any reasonable standards, it would seem that Nolan should be satisfied, but on the contrary, his lust for land, and for the power which comes with it, had increased in direct ratio to the number of acres under his thumb. Now there were only six small ranches left within a twenty-five mile radius of Holbrook, and it was about these survivors that Nolan and his hired gun were talking. Actually, Nolan was doing most of the talking, with Dakota Groves nodding from time to time to indicate that he understood.

Their conversation was taking place in what had been designed to be the parlor of the Slash N ranch house, a huge room which, had there been a woman in charge, could have been made elegant, but which was so cluttered with discarded ranch gear and other odds and ends that it looked like a junk shop. Even Nolan's big desk was almost buried under a mountain of cattleman's journals and week-old Kansas City newspapers. Dakota Groves, had he thought about it at all, might well have wondered how anybody who was as meticulous as Nolan about his personal appearance could endure such disorder.

Groves, however, was more intrigued by something Nolan had just said, and he ventured to ask a question which had puzzled him for some time.

"It's none of my business, boss, but how come you're so all-fired anxious to get hold of Ben Gibson's place? I mean when Lew Jennings' Box J is half again as big, and has a spring on it to boot."

Nolan didn't like having his motives questioned,

but neither did he want to antagonize Groves, so he said with a shrug, "Call it just a notion. Anyway, Gibson's Double X is the one I want first. Jennings' turn will come later."

It wasn't much of an answer, but Dakota Groves knew better than to press the point. He simply asked, "What do you want me to do about it?"

"Nothing... yet," Nolan told him. "But just be sure you're ready when the time comes. I'll let you know."

Groves nodded, and when it became apparent that Nolan considered the subject closed, turned and left the room. It crossed his mind that the boss might be more interested in Gibson's daughter than in his ranch.

Groves was wrong about Nolan's having an eye for Laura Gibson, but his guess wasn't too far off target at that. There really was a woman involved, only it was Ellen Troup instead of Laura Gibson. Nolan was still smarting from the rebuff Ellen had given him at the restaurant. He wasn't used to playing second fiddle to anyone, let alone a small town sheriff who probably didn't own much more than a horse and the clothes on his back. How any woman in her right mind could choose Durham over the wealthiest rancher in the territory was beyond Nolan's comprehension. he could buy a dozen sheriffs!

Still, Nolan was no fool. He knew that Ed Durham was one sheriff who couldn't be bought. Neither could he be scared. This left only one choice; he had to be killed. But the killing had to be done in such a way that it couldn't possibly be tied to Nolan, or to anyone in his employ, including

Dakota Groves. Which was where Ben Gibson came into the picture. Gibson and the sheriff were friends. Also, Gibson was respected and liked by the other small ranchers, and if anyone could unite them, he was the man to do it. Of course even united they would be no match for Nolan, who had a carefully selected crew of twenty, none of them quite as good with a gun as Dakota Groves, but all of them far more dangerous than the ranchers, some of whom were well along in years. And if open warfare broke out, carefully planned by Nolan so as to appear as if the small ranchers had started it, Sheriff Durhm would have to get involved.

Nolan's lips quirked in an anticipatory smile. In a range war men got shot, even men wearing badges. If the Sheriff caught a stray bullet, there would be no way of determining who had fired it. And with the sheriff out of the way, the little ranchers could be wiped out. Then Slash N would control the whole range, and he, Nolan, would have smooth sailing insofar as Ellen Troup was concerned.

The mental picture was so satisfying that Nolan was smiling as he sat down at his desk, took a cigar out of his pocket, and lit it. When the time was ripe. . . He frowned. Wait a minute! Why put it off? Al Gregg, the deputy, had been killed last night. Word of this had been brought to Nolan by one of his men who had been in the saloon when it had happened. Now was the time to strike, while the sheriff was short-handed. Knowing Durham as he did, Nolan was satisfied that if trouble broke out, the man would go into action, crippled or not.

Never one to procrastinate, Nolan got up and hurried out of the house. Dakota Groves was at the corral, getting ready to drop his loop on a horse. He heard the door bang, turned to see Nolan beckoning him, and headed back to the house, coiling his rope as he walked.

Nolan waited for him to come close, took a careful look around, although he knew the rest of the crew, except for the Chinese cook, was out on the range, and said deliberately, "I've got a hunch that Ben Gibson has been eating Slash N beef again. Of course he'd ditch the hides, since they're wearing my brand. Most likely in that little gully that crosses his place, where he could cover them with rocks."

Groves frowned for a moment, then a look of comprehension showed on his face.

"Sounds reasonable, boss. thing to do, steal another man's cattle. Want me to go take a look?"

"Not right now," Nolan said. "But tomorrow morning I'm going into town and tell the sheriff. He'll want proof. This time he'll find it. Right?"

"Sure thing, boss," Groves said, and went back to the corral. Nolan watched him rope out a horse and lead it to the barn. When Groves rode off, headed west, where the rest of the crew were working, Nolan smiled with satisfaction. Groves knew what he was supposed to do. And he was smart enough to wait until dark to do it.

Unaware of what was being planned at Slash N, Ben Gibson was hitching a horse to a buckboard, so that his girl Laura could drive into town. Laura was perfectly capable of doing the harnessing herself, and would ordinarily have done so. For that matter, she was as good at all types of ranch work as most men, and better than some, having been reared right there on Double X. Today, however, she wasn't dressed for such work. Al Gregg's funeral was to be held this noon, and she was going to attend. She and Al had not been really close, although he would have liked it that way, but they had enjoyed each other's company, and she had felt a sense of loss since hearing of his death.

Her father, a stocky, usually amiable man in his early fifties, turned to watch her come out of the house, and his face lit up as it always did when she was around. He took the ever-present pipe out of his mouth and said appreciatively, "You look mighty pretty in that dress, girl. Too pretty to be going to a funeral."

"Thank you, kind sir," Laura said, smiling and making a mock curtsy. Then the smile faded, and she said more soberly, "Actually, it isn't the kind of dress you usually associate with funerals, but as you know, it's the only one I have. To tell the truth, I'd feel more comfortable in my Levi's and a flannel shirt, but you can imagine what folks would say if I showed up dressed like that."

Her father nodded, waited for her to step up onto the buckboard, and handed her the lines.

"Wish I could go with you, but you know how it is. We don't dare both leave the ranch at the same time. It might give ideas to some of those no-goods Nolan has working for him. I wish. . ."

"Wish *what*, Pa?"

"Nothing," Ben said, forcing a grin. "You be careful, girl. Give my regards to any of our friends you see. Any idea what time you'll get back?"

"It may be pretty late," Laura said. "I intend to do a little visiting, maybe pick up some gossip. Don't worry about me; I can take care of myself."

"Sure you can," her father said. "But just in case, I shoved the shotgun under the seat."

Laura jiggled the lines, and the buckboard moved away. The horse was eager, and Laura didn't try to hold him back, although she kept a tight grip on the lines in case the animal should get too frisky.

Driving was second nature to her, the same as riding, and didn't require much concentration, so she had time to think about her father's unfinished sentence. She could guess the rest of it; he wished Nolan and all his crew would disappear from the face of the earth, and things could be like they once were. It was a sentiment with which she agreed heartily. Nolan had been nothing but trouble for the small ranches like Double X for the last dozen years. She could remember when she, as a child, had watched her playmates ride away on wagons loaded with all their families' possessions. Although she never talked about it, she dreaded the day when Nolan would decide to put pressure on the Double X. She was sure her father couldn't be coerced or frightened into moving. He'd stay and fight, regardless of the odds.

Nolan had already made his first move by accusing her father of stealing some Slash N calves. His accusation had brought the sheriff to the ranch, albeit reluctantly. Of course he had found no evidence, because there had been none to find. Nolan had passed it off as a misunderstanding based on faulty information he claimed to have received, but he had not apologized. She doubted that Nolan would ever apologize for anything. In his eyes he was King, and the King could do no wrong.

The buckboard topped a small rise, and she saw Holbrook sprawled in front of her. Townsfolk were already clustered around the schoolhouse, which served as a church on Sundays or special occasions such as this. A little guiltily, she recalled the times when she, as one of the pupils, had been elated at getting an unscheduled holiday, even one which was due to a funeral.

Today she felt none of that pleasant excitement. It was sad when a young man like Al Gregg, with a long life presumably ahead of him, could be cut down by a murderer's bullet.

She pulled the buckboard off to the right side of the road, and handed the lines to one of the men who reached for them. After watching him attach the weight to the bridle, and thanking him for his help, she joined the group in front of the school building.

Many of her friends were there, including some of the small ranchers and their wives. They all welcomed her with properly subdued pleasure, and by then it was time to go into the temporary church. The service, conducted by a white-haired retired Baptist preacher, was mercifully short, and afterward, all those who could, accompanied the coffin to the graveyard. Laura was not surprised that neither Nolan nor any of his hired hands had deigned to attend, although some of them must have known Al.

Leaving the graveyard, everyone seemed to take a deep breath and relax. Laura was greeted warmly from all sides, and Ellen Troup, who had closed the restaurant for the funeral, invited her to come there a little later for dinner. Laura liked Ellen, but had to decline the invitation as she had already accepted one from a long time friend and former schoolmate who lived in town. The girl's name had been Elaine Cogswell, but she was now Mrs. Horace Trimble, wife of Rex Bates' bank clerk, and by looking at her you could guess that there would soon be a third member in the Trimble family.

On the way to the Trimble house, they stopped to speak to Sheriff Durham, who was talking to a stranger not much older than Laura.

"I'd like you to meet my new deputy, Martin Davis," the sheriff said. "Martin, this is Laura Gibson. I believe you've already met Mrs. Trimble."

"A pleasure, Miss Gibson," Matt said, removing his hat. "I've heard the sheriff mention your father."

Laura found herself looking at the new deputy with interest. She was mentally trying to visualize him as he might look without his beard. He seemed to be regarding her with more than casual attention, and both of them averted their eyes quickly as the sheriff said, "I trust your pa's all right?"

"Pa? Oh yes, he's fine. He said to give you his regards. Come out to the ranch when you have a chance."

"I'll do that," the sheriff promised. "But not for a week or two. My leg's still bothering me a bit."

Laura and her friend moved on then, and when they were out of earshot, Elaine asked, "What do you think of Martin Davis?"

"Who? Oh, the deputy. He seems nice enough." She tried to keep it casual, but Elaine's soft laugh told her that she had failed. Embarrassed, she hurried to a safer subject. "I'm dying to hear what's been going on in town since my last visit. Tell me about yourself first. Are you hoping for a boy or for a girl?"

"A girl," Elaine said without hesitation. "And if it is, I'm going to name her Laura after you. If you don't mind, that is."

"I'd love it," Laura said enthusiastically. "Does Horace want a girl, too?"

"He says he'll settle for either one, providing it's soon. You know how men are."

"Not really," Laura said. "About the only man I see regularly is Pa, except on these rare occasions when I come to town. Now tell me all the gossip. You must have some juicy tidbits, haven't you?"

This was all Elaine needed to start her off. As a result, Laura was later than she had intended leaving for home. She knew her father would be worrying about her, and she would have driven faster, but it got dark, and she didn't want to risk breaking a wheel in a pothole.

It didn't occur to her to be afraid. Not, that was, until she came within a mile of the ranch, and heard a horse snuffle. She called out, but there was no answer, and this really worried her. Anyone was entitled to use this road, but why had her greeting been ignored?

A little self-consciously, she reached under the seat for the shotgun. At that moment she saw the horseman, silhouetted blackly against the sky. He seemed to be waiting for her.

Chapter Nine

Laura's father, as Laura had surmised, had been worrying about her. He usually did when she was out of his sight for any length of time. It was a habit he wanted to break, for he realized that she was no longer the little girl to whom he had tried to be both father and mother since the death of his wife eleven years ago. He was justly proud of the results of his handiwork, for Laura, in addition to being physically attractive, was level-headed, and had a cheerful disposition. Also, as she had pointed out, she could take care of herself.

Nevertheless, he sighed with relief when he heard the buckboard approaching, its iron-tired wheels crunching the gravel of the ranchyard. He hurried to the barn, lit a lantern hanging from a rafter, and was waiting when Laura drove in.

Laura smiled at him, but her smile was a bit forced, and he asked quickly, "Are you all right?"

"I'm fine," Laura assured him, and then, because she and her father never lied to each other, "Maybe a little scared, to tell the truth. Oh, it's nothing serious, just something I can't understand. I'll tell you about it in the house."

Ben didn't persist, but quickly unharnessed the horse and put it in its stall. He had already taken care of its feed and water, so all he had to do was rub it down and push the buckboard to its usual place in the back of the barn, after which he took down the lantern and hurried to the house, anxious to learn what had happened. Laura had said that it was nothing serious, but she had admitted to being scared, and she didn't scare easily.

Laura had already discarded her finery, and was wearing jeans and a wool shirt. She turned from the stove, on which she had moved the big coffeepot to a hotter spot, and asked in a conversational tone, "Have you had any supper?"

"Yes. I made myself a sandwich and warmed up those left-over beans from last night. How about you?"

"Elaine Trimble insisted on my eating before I left. We had a lot of talking to do. Mostly about her baby, which according to Doc Yarborough, is due in two months. You know how she and I are when we get together; we don't know when to stop. Oh, the sheriff sends you his regards. He already has a new deputy. Several others of our friends asked to be remembered to you."

"Suppose you tell me that part later," her father suggested. "Right now I'm more interested in finding out what scared you."

Before answering, Laura poured two cups of coffee, placed them on the kitchen table, and sat down. She waited for her father to take the chair opposite her, then said, "Well, as I've already told you, it was more confusing than frightening. When I was almost home, probably less than a mile from here, a rider loomed up out of the darkness."

Her father set his cup down so suddenly that a little coffee splashed over. In a tense voice he demanded, "Did he give you any trouble?"

"He'd better *not* have!" Laura said, smiling. "Not when I had the shotgun in my lap, though of course he couldn't see it in the dark. He may have recognized my voice, I suppose."

"What did he say?"

"That's just it. He didn't say a word. If he intended to, he must have changed his mind, because when I brought the buckboard to a stop, he whirled his horse and took off."

Her father didn't comment immediately, but reached for his pipe and stuck the stem in his mouth. The action was purely mechanical, for he never smoked in the house, a habit which he had established many years before when his wife had been afflicted with weak lungs, and which had stayed with him ever since. After a bit he took the pipe out of his mouth.

"I don't suppose you recognized the man?"

Laura shook her head.

"It could have been anyone."

"No," her father said. "Not *anyone*. It had to be somebody whose voice you would have known. That's why he didn't answer you."

"I hadn't thought of that," Laura admitted. "But what difference could it have made? He had as much right on the road as I had. I hadn't even reached the edge of our property, so he wasn't trespassing. I just can't understand it."

"Neither can I," her father acknowledged. "But I don't like it. If he'd been a friend of ours, he would have identified himself. Which means he *wasn't* a friend, but was still somebody whose voice would've given him away. To my way of thinking, that makes him an enemy. And the only person I've had trouble with is Nolan." He lifted his hand to forestall a protest. "No, I don't think it was Nolan himself, but it could have been one of those owlhoots he has working for him."

"But why?" Laura asked, beginning to share her father's uneasiness. "I mean even assuming that he was one of the Slash N crew, he hadn't done anything, had he? You were right here all the time. I can't see. . . "

"Nor can I," her father said, interrupting her. "But I sure as blazes aim to find out."

"You're not going to go charging over to Slash N and accuse Nolan!"

"No. I'm not that crazy. But come daylight, I'll do some checking around. If the feller was as close as that to our land, he may have been *on* it, and if he was, he must've left some kind of tracks. His horse would, I mean. Unless it had wings."

"I think we can rule out that possibility," Laura said, smiling. "It was hoofbeats I heard when he rode off, not wings flapping. Anyway, there's nothing we can do about it until morning. Let me fill your cup again, and then I'll pass along a few of the things Elaine told me. Some of them will make your eyes pop. You know that mousy Thelma Dunning?"

"Gossip!" her father said, shaking his head, but grinning at the same time. "All right, but take it easy, will you? Remember, I've got very delicate ears."

The town of Holbrook, with al Gregg's funeral a day in the past, had settled back into its customary rut. The next break in routine would be the trial of Gregg's killer, who still refused to identify himself, even though there was good reason to believe that he was the bank robber from New Mexico whose name on the notice was given as Roy Willey, along with several aliases. Since Judge Jensen wasn't due on his circuit for two days, the sheriff was stuck with Willey at least that long. Perhaps longer, although in view of the preponderance of evidence, the sheriff anticipated a speedy trial.

Meanwhile, there was no choice but to endure the man's company, and listen to his incessant grumbling. The cell was cold, the bunk too narrow, the food inedible. This last complaint was ridiculous, for the prisoner's meals were prepared at the restaurant by Ellen Troup, and were undoubtedly twice as good as Willey, or whoever he really was, was used to.

By now it was apparent to the sheriff that his new deputy had no inkling of their blood relationship. Martin. . . it was hard not to think of him as Matt. . . gave every indication of being able to handle the job as well as, if not better than, his predecessor. If any of the merchants had been a little leery because of the violence associated with his arrival in Holbrook, their uneasiness vanished when he was introduced to them by the sheriff, and proved to be polite and unassuming, not at all trigger happy.

The town's reaction was so favorable, in fact, that the sheriff wished he could let the world know that Matt was his son. Since this would have been disastrous, it had to remain a secret. Except from Ellen, of course, who could be counted on not to give it away.

The two lawmen were in the cafe, having their noon meal, when Matt, who was facing the door, remarked, "Seems you have a visitor. A man I haven't seen before just tied up at your rail, and tried the door. Now he's peeking in the window. Should I go over and find out what he wants?"

The sheriff turned to look over his shoulder, frowned, and said soberly, "We'll both go. That's Nolan, the rancher I told you about who owns Slash N nine miles south of town. I don't know what he wants, but I'd lay even money it means trouble. He was in to see me day before yesterday, and he wouldn't be back just on a social visit. Let's go. I want to head him off before he comes here looking for me."

Matt didn't understand this last statement, of course, nor could he interpret the look which passed between the sheriff and Ellen Troup, but he immediately stood up, and followed the sheriff out of the cafe. He didn't have to stop at the till, for he had already made arrangements with Ellen to pay for his meals on a weekly basis.

Nolan, who had turned away from the office window, watched them approach. His expression was hard to read, but it was certainly not a smile. He did, however, unbend enough to acknowledge the sheriff's introduction of Matt as "my new deputy, Martin Davis," before concentrating his attention on the sheriff and saying curtly, "You told me to come back when I had proof. Well, this time I have. If you'll come along, you can see for yourself." He glanced at the sheriff's cane, and added pointedly, "Provided you're able to ride, that is."

The sheriff's lips tightened, but he ignored the slur and said without emotion, "Before we talk about riding, suppose you tell me just what's supposed to have happened, and what kind of evidence you claim to have."

Nolan's face flushed with anger.

"~~Damn it~~, you know who I'm talking about. Ben Gibson has helped himself to a couple more of my calves, and this time one of my men saw him do it."

The sheriff looked up quickly.

"Was there any shooting?"

"No. My man kept out of sight. But he watched Gibson cache the hides. Well, are you coming, or aren't you?"

"I'm not," the sheriff said.

Nolan looked both angry and surprised.

"~~Damn it~~, Durham, you're supposed..."

"Hold it!" the sheriff cut in. "I'm not going, but I'm sending my deputy. Any objections?"

Nolan was obviously unprepared for this. Finally he shrugged, and said stiffly, "That'll have to do, I suppose." He turned away, untied his horse, and swung up into the saddle.

The sheriff faced Matt, and said loudly enough for Nolan to hear, "You don't know Ben Gibson, and you've just met Nolan for the first time, so nobody can accuse you of being partial. Go take a look and report back. Okay?"

"Yes, sir," Matt said, and went for his horse, which had been re-shod, and was tied in the shade behind the jail. Moments later he rode into sight, lifted a hand to the sheriff, and rode away alongside Nolan.

For the first mile Nolan maintained a tight-lipped silence. Then he asked imperiously without turning his head, "How long have you been a lawman?"

87

Matt deliberately delayed his answer until Nolan turned to face him, then said laconically, "Long enough to know a calf hide when I see one, and to read a brand. I reckon that's all that's necessary at the moment, isn't it?"

Nolan didn't answer, but spurred his horse and drew away. Matt eased his own mount into a canter, and caught up. They were riding abreast again when a buckboard came toward them. Matt didn't recognize the driver, but the horse and rig were familiar. It was the one driven to the funeral by the girl who had been introduced to him as Laura Gibson.

The two riders reined up as the wagon reached them and came to a stop. The driver, a stocky man whom Matt presumed to be Ben Gibson, glanced briefly at Matt, then scowled at Nolan. He looked angry enough to explode, but instead of addressing himself to the rancher, said unexpectedly, "Deputy, I'd appreciate it if you'd look under the canvas in the back of this buckboard."

Matt, completely puzzled, rode close enough to reach down and take hold of the canvas. He flipped it aside, and revealed two fresh calf hides with bits of flesh still clinging to them. The probable significance dawned on him, and he turned to look at Nolan, at the same time letting his hand edge toward his gun. He didn't know Nolan well enough to gauge how he would react, but it seemed like a touchy situation.

If Nolan had a gun, he didn't reach for it, but his face was like a thundercloud, and his voice a whiplash.

"What the hell are you trying to prove, Gibson?"

Gibson, not at all intimidated by Nolan's threatening attitude, said evenly, "You already know the answer to that, but for the benefit of this young man, who must be the deputy my daughter told me about, I'll lay it on the line. You killed a couple of your own branded calves, and hid the hides on my ranch, figuring to put the blame on me. It might've worked, too, if the fool who did it had hightailed back to your ranch. But he didn't, and my daughter saw him. This morning I picked up his trail, and back-tracked it to where he'd ditched the hides. I'm on my way to town now, to show them to the sheriff."

"That's a lie!" Nolan snapped. With obvious distaste, he was forced to appeal to Matt.

"You see what he's up to, don't you, Deputy? We caught him red-handed, and he's trying to lie his way out of it. I demand that you arrest him."

Matt would not have chosen to get involved in an affair about which he knew so little, but Nolan's arrogance was too much for him. He said shortly, "I take my orders from the sheriff, Mr. Nolan. Besides, I'm not sure Mr. Gibson is lying. Not unless someone can explain why he'd be taking the hides to Holbrook, if he'd actually killed your calves. I suggest that we all go to town and hear what the sheriff has to say."

"Suits me," Gibson said.

"Well, it doesn't suit me," Nolan said viciously. "This shirttail rancher and Durham are long time friends. The sheriff would back him up regardless of the evidence."

"You're entitled to your opinion," Matt said. "But I don't have to agree with it. I happen to believe that the sheriff is an honorable man."

"I don't give a damn what you believe!" Nolan growled. "As far as I'm concerned, you're a nobody. You blow into town in time to kill a man who isn't even shooting at you, and all of a sudden you're a hero. Don't let it go to your head!"

He seemed about to say more, but if so changed his mind, whirled his horse on its haunches, and took off, presumably toward Slash N.

Matt was hot under the collar, and he was surprised to find Ben Gibson grinning.

"Nolan sort of got to you, didn't he?" the owner of Double X said. "He ain't used to being stood up to. Figures he's God or something." The grin faded, and he added soberly, "I wouldn't take it too lightly, though. He's a bad man to have for an enemy. I hope you don't get into trouble on account of standing up for me."

"I've been in trouble before," Matt shrugged, in an understatement. "Well, do you still want to go to town?"

"Don't reckong it'll be necessary now," Gibson said, tamping tobacco into his pipe. "You can tell it to the sheriff the way you saw it. When he feels like coming out to the ranch, I'll show him where I found the hides. Or you can come yourself, if you like. It'd be nice for Laura to have someone her own age to talk to."

"Thanks, I might do that if it's all right with the sheriff," Matt said, and watched Gibson turn the buckboard and head back the way he had come. It occurred to Matt that he just might accept the invitation. Since meeting Laura after the funeral, he hadn't been able to get her out of his mind.

Chapter Ten

When her father drove into the ranch yard, Laura came out of the barn. She had a pitchfork in her hand, and there were a few wisps of hay clinging to her Levi's, so she had obviously been pitching feed from the loft down into the stalls.

"You made a quick trip, Pa. I hope you didn't hurry back on my account. I've been keeping the shotgun close at hand in case we had any unwelcome visitors."

"Good idea," her father said approvingly. "But what happened was that I didn't have to go all the way into town. I met Nolan and that young deputy on the road. They were headed for this place. Like we guessed, Nolan was fixing to frame me for killing his calves. He'd already reported it to the sheriff."

"What happened? Out on the road, I mean."

"Well, before Nolan could say anything, I asked the deputy. . . Davis, did you say his name was?"

"Martin Davis."

"Yes. Well, I asked him to take a look in the back of the buckboard, where I had the hides. It sort of caught Nolan off balance."

"I bet it did! What did he say?"

"Oh, you know Nolan. He still claimed I'd

stolen the calves. He ordered the deputy to arrest me." Gibson grinned at the memory. "You should've seen Nolan's face when Davis told him he took his orders from the sheriff. Not only that, Davis also said it seemed unlikely to him that if I'd done what Nolan accused me of, I'd be hauling the evidence to town. That deputy may be new on the job, and sort of young, but he's got a cool head. Didn't fly off the handle when Nolan gave him a tongue lashing, just let it slide off his shoulders. Not that he wasn't sore; you could tell that by looking at him, but he cooled off as soon as Nolan lit out for Slash N."

"I'm glad it was no worse," Laura said. "I'm afraid if I'd been there I would have given Nolan a piece of my mind. Imagine accusing you of a thing like that!"

"It's been coming for a long time," her father said. "Nolan's bound and determined to take over every ranch in the county. Or in the territory, for all I know. I still can't figure out, though, why he picked this place for his next target. There's bigger ranches just as easy to grab. Like Lew Jennings' Box J, for instance." He looked at Laura in sudden concern. "Nolan hasn't been making any advances, has he?"

"Goodness no! He probably doesn't even know I'm alive."

"I doubt that, girl. There ain't a man around who doesn't turn his head when you walk by. I've looked in on a couple of Saturday night dances at the school house, and I ain't exactly blind."

"You're imagining things," Laura said, but she couldn't help looking pleased.

"Maybe, and maybe not. Oh, by the way, I

invited that deputy to come out and see where I found the hides. Him and the sheriff both, if Ed's up to riding this far with his bum leg."

Laura didn't comment, but instinctively reached up to brush back a lock of hair which had fallen across her forehead. She looked at her father soberly.

"What do you suppose Nolan will try next?"

"I don't know. But there's something I *do* know. If us small ranchers don't get together, Nolan will gobble us up one by one. Is there a stall ready for this horse?"

"Not quite," Laura said. "I didn't expect you back so soon, so I was doing some other things first."

"Then I'll put him in the corral with the others." He got down off the seat and began unbuckling the harness.

Laura went back into the barn to continue her work, but her mind wasn't on it. When her father came back from the corral, and entered the barn, she looked at him over the side of the stall in which she was working.

"You said something about the small ranchers getting together. Do you really think that's possible? I mean the others are pretty independent, the same as you. And even if you could work out some kind of arrangement, Nolan would have us outnumbered. He must have close to two dozen men working for him, most of them the sort you wouldn't want to meet in a dark alley. How many of our friends do you think would be brave enough to stand up to him?"

"Well, I would, for one. Then there's Lew Jennings, who I just mentioned. He's got one man working for him, and his oldest boy must be close on to sixteen. That makes four."

"Go on," Laura prompted. "Who else?"

"All right, Dutch Schloemp. I know he's sort of standoffish, being a foreigner and everything, but he's strong as a bull, and I don't figure him as a coward. If he came in with us, so would his two sons. And Nels Nordquest."

"Who is sixty years old," Laura said. "I don't mean to be a wet blanket, but even if everybody went along with your idea, we'd end up with a bunch of men and boys who know lots about cattle but not much about guns."

"I notice you keep saying 'we,' " her father said. "I'm not letting you get mixed up in anything."

"If you're in, I'm in," Laura said positively. "I'm no better than Dutch Schloemp's boys, or Lew Jennings and his sons, and I can shoot as straight as any of them."

"Dammit, girl. . ."

"You know I'm right," Laura said. "And of course *you're* right, too. We can't just wait for Nolan to pick us off one at a time. It's just that I hate the idea of a war."

"Me, too, but I wasn't so crazy about being accused of calf stealing, either. Why, except for you seeing that rider last night, Nolan's scheme might have worked, and I'd be in jail right now."

"Don't even *think* about it," Laura said. "All right, how do you intend to start?"

"I've been studying on that while I was driving home. I think I'll talk first to Lew Jennings. He's got a good head on his shoulders. Maybe he'll have a better idea than mine. I reckon I'll saddle up and ride over there right now. Unless you need me around here, that is."

"You go ahead," Laura said. "Since your mind's made up, there's nothing to be gained by putting it off."

"That's exactly how I feel. I'll try to get back before dark, but you keep that shotgun handy."

Laura nodded, and watched him saddle a dun gelding and ride off. She tried to turn her thoughts from what this might lead to, and found herself thinking about the new deputy. If he came out, she hoped he wouldn't find her looking like *this*.

Lew Jennings wasn't at the Box J ranch house, but his wife, Martha, saw Ben Gibson from her kitchen window, and came out to greet him, drying her hands on a dish towel. Her welcoming smile was warm enough, but Gibson thought she looked worried, and her first words proved him right.

"It's been a long time, Ben. I hope there's nothing wrong. Is Laura all right?"

"Frisky as a filly," Ben assured her. He grinned. "Can't a neighbor drop by without there being something wrong?"

"Of course, Martha Jennings said, laughing. "But you have to admit that it's unusual, seeing you in the middle of the afternoon. Not that I don't wish you and Laura would come around oftener."

"We mean to, but there's always something that has to be done. Any idea where I'd find Lew?"

"He's out at the dirt water tank, him and both the boys. They've been working on it all day. I don't know what happened, but one side of the tank burst out."

"The dirt tank?" Gibson asked, frowning. "I never knew one of those to give way. Not unless we had a cloudburst or something."

"Lew said the same thing. He couldn't figure it out, either. Of course most of the water had spilled out before he knew about it, so there wasn't any way to tell how it started."

"Likely the dirt wasn't tamped down hard enough," Gibson said. "Well, I'll go have a look at it myself. You and Lew come over when you get a chance. Bring the boys."

Martha nodded, and Ben rode off toward the water tank. What he had said about it not being tamped down hard enough had been intended to relieve Martha's mind, but he didn't believe it for a minute. Her husband wasn't a sloppy worker. He would have done the job right.

Jennings and his two boys had finished the repairs, and were just starting back toward the house when Ben met them. Jennings was a tall, raw boned man of about fifty, with a drooping mustache at which he tugged when he was agitated. The two men exchanged salutations, and Ben grinned at Jennings' sons: Rafe, who was about sixteen, and Billy, some three years younger.

"Lordy, you boys are shooting up like weeds. You'll soon be taller than your pa."

The boys grinned back at him, and Rafe said respectfully, "Not likely, Mr. Gibson. Pa's six feet two."

"You'll make it," Ben predicted. "Both of you." He turned his attention to Lew.

"Your missus tells me you've had some trouble with your water tank. Long as I'm here, I'd like to look at it. Why don't you send the boys on home, and you and me will ride back."

Lew looked at him thoughtfully for a moment,

then said to his sons, "You two go on. Your ma likely has some chores for you. We won't be far behind."

The boys rode off, making a race of it, and Lew said soberly, "What was that business about sending the boys on ahead? Have you got something to say that you didn't want them to hear?"

Ben nodded.

"No point getting them excited. Nolan butchered a couple of his own calves and hid the hides on Double X. He intended to make out I was a cattle thief. It didn't work out that way, for reasons I'll go into when I have time. The point is, he's trying to force me out, like he did the others that have left. Or got killed. Do you follow me?"

"I'm way ahead of you," Lew said. "But keep talking. I know you didn't ride over here to cry on my shoulder. What was your real reason?"

"I want all of us small ranchers to get together," Ben said. "Otherwise we'll be wiped out one at a time. Don't you agree?"

Jennings began tugging at his mustache, which was not an encouraging sign.

"I do and I don't. Oh, I know what Nolan wants, and it scares the pee-waddin' out of me, but I also know something about range wars. I was in the middle of one up in Wyoming a good many years ago. It was plain hell. Innocent men killed, houses burned, other things I don't even like to think about."

There was no answer to this, so Gibson held his silence. After a bit Jennings quit fooling with his mustache, met Gibson's eyes, and said heavily, "All right, Ben, I agree with you. Partly because I have confidence in your judgement, and partly on account of what happened to my water tank. You know and I know that a dirt tank doesn't crumble of its own accord. Not when it's been checked properly at the end of the winter. I inspected mine not over a month ago, and it was as good as new. Somebody deliberately gouged a hole in it."

"Nolan?" Ben asked, and Lew nodded.

"Nobody else had any reason to. You know me. I don't go looking for trouble. Far as I know, I haven't made any enemies. I've even tried to get along with Nolan, when I really knew it was no use. I reckon it's time I quit fooling myself. How do you aim to go about this?"

Ben Gibson felt no elation at having won Jennings over to his way of thinking. Jennings, having made up his mind, would stand by his decision. If things went wrong, it could cost him his ranch. Or worse; he or one or both of his boys could be killed. Maybe it had been a mistake, dragging him into it. Maybe. . . But no, it was still true that unless the small ranchers united, they wouldn't stand a chance. Nolan had been nibbling away at them for years. His latest action, trying to make Ben look like a cattle thief, indicated that he was getting impatient.

"I figure the first thing is to talk to the other small ranchers. Besides you and me, there's Dutch Schloemp, Nels Nordquest, Hank Debrow, and Will Otis. Those are all we've got left. Of course there's the nesters, but they won't take sides. I'd rather you and me could go together to see the others, but we can save time by splitting up. I'll visit Dutch and Nordquest. Will you talk to the other two?"

"Yes," Jennings said. "I'll ride out to their places tonight after dark."

"Good," Ben said. "We don't want to attract too much attention. I'll do the same for my two. What do you think about all of us getting together Saturday night? There'll be more folks moving around then, and we won't be so noticeable. We can meet at my place, if that's all right with everybody. Say nine o'clock?"

"The time and place are okay," Jennings said. "Getting them there is another matter. They're all scared of Nolan. So am I, if you want the God's honest truth."

"Don't think you're alone in that respect," Gibson said. "I'm as scared as you are, not only for myself, but for Laura. And you've got two sons and Martha to think about. Speaking of which, we'd better be getting back to your place or they'll start wondering what happened to us."

"Do you still want to see the water tank?"

"No, that was just an excuse to talk to you alone."

They turned their horses toward the Box J headquarters, riding in silence until they were almost at the ranch yard. Then Ben asked, "Are you going to tell your missus about this?"

"Sure," Jennings said. "She'll guess something's up as soon as she sees my face. After thirty-five years together, she can read me like a book. The boys will have to know, too. We're all in this together. If it comes to a showdown, Rafe will be right alongside me. God! I hate to think of him getting shot."

"I know," Ben said. "Laura says she's part of it, too." He looked around at his friend. "You can still back out, if you want to. Nobody'll blame you."

"No," Jennings stated flatly. "I said I was in, and I am. I just hope it won't end up like the affair in Wyoming."

"It won't," Ben declared, with more confidence than he felt. "Before I'd let that happen, I'd go kill Nolan, even if it meant shooting him from ambush."

"No," Jennings said, and for the first time, he smiled. "You won't do that, Ben, because it ain't your nature. If you went after Nolan, it'd be face to face. And of course you'd end up dead. He doesn't keep all those men around him for their looks. How about coming in for a cup of coffee?"

"Thanks just the same, but I'd better be getting home. I'll try to check with you tomorrow, to see how you come out with Debrow and Otis. Tell Martha and the boys goodbye for me. Oh, one more thing; how about that man you have working for you? Will he come in with us?"

"Slater. I reckon so, but don't count on it too much. He sort of keeps his thoughts to himself. He might not want to get involved. I'll talk to him, of course, when the time comes."

"Good," Ben said. "So long until tomorrow."

"So long," Jennings echoed. He watched Gibson ride off, then squared his shoulders and rode on toward the house, where Martha would be waiting. She'd know something was up, and he dreaded telling her what it was.

Chapter Eleven

Matt rode back to Holbrook, wondering if the sheriff would approve of the way he had handled the confrontation between Nolan and Ben Gibson. For some reason, the sheriff's approbation was very important to him. He didn't know why. Certainly not out of fear of losing his job, which he considered only temporary at best. And he hadn't been in Holbrook long enough to form any personal attachment to the place, or to any of its citizens. Not even to Sheriff Durham, although there was no denying that he liked the man. He liked Ellen Troup, too. She and the sheriff would make a good pair. He wondered why they hadn't married.

Damn it, what business was it of his? He gigged his horse, entered Holbrook's main street, dismounted in front of the sheriff's office, and went in.

There was no sign of the sheriff, but from the back of the room, the prisoner called, "Hey, Deputy. Come back here! I want to talk to you."

Matt hesitated a second, then walked far enough to ascertain that the cell was still secure. Before going any farther, he drew his pistol and laid it on the floor. He didn't want anyone pulling on him the trick that he had used against the marshal in Gunnison.

"All right, what do you want? If you've got any complaints about the way you're being treated, save your breath."

"Me complain? Where did you get that idea? I just want to ask you a question. How would you like to pick up an easy thousand bucks?"

Matt shrugged without answering, and the prisoner hurried on, lowering his voice to a conspiratorial whisper.

"You're probably thinking that I haven't got a thousand dollars, and you're right. Not on me, or that stinkin' sheriff would've found it. But I know where it is, make no mistake about that. Are you interested, or ain't you?"

"Anyone would be interested in a thousand dollars," Matt said, without committing himself. "What would I have to do to get it? Unlock the cell and let you go? You must think I'm crazy. Besides, I'm pretty sure you're lying. Where would a saddlebum like you get his hands on that kind of money? I bet you haven't seen that much in your life. On second thought, I'm not interested after all." He made as though to turn away.

"Wait! You haven't heard it all. Supposing, just supposing, I knew where the feller that robbed that New Mexico bank hid the loot. And supposing. . . "

"While you're doing all this supposing," Matt cut in, "suppose you tell me where it is, and let me go see for myself."

"Damn it, you know I ain't going to do that."

"I didn't expect you to," Matt said. "I told you

I was interested, and I was, but not in the idea of making a thousand dollars. If there had ever been any doubt about you being the man wanted in New Mexico, what you've just told me wiped it out. The sheriff will be glad to hear about it. The judge, too, for that matter."

"Why you double-crossing bastard!"

"Thanks. I like you, too," Matt said. He picked up his pistol, slid it into its holster, and returned to the front of the room to look out the door.

The sheriff was coming from the direction of the mercantile, carrying his cane, but not using it. He had of course noticed Matt's horse at the tie rail, so was not surprised to find Matt waiting for him. Matt stepped aside to let him pass, and waited for him to open the conversation, which he did after getting settled behind his desk.

"You're back sooner than I expected. Tell me about it."

"Yes, sir."

Matt reported what had happened on the road, while the sheriff listened without comment, although he smiled when Matt told about finding the calf hides in the back of Gibson's buckboard. The smile vanished, however, as Matt reported Nolan's reaction to his refusal to arrest Gibson.

"That's about all, Sheriff. Nolan took off like a turpentined dog, and Mr. Gibson went back to the ranch. I like Gibson, by the way, which is more than I can say about Nolan."

"That's understandable," the sheriff said. "You handled the situation as well as I could have."

"Thank you," Matt said, greatly pleased.

The sheriff smiled wryly.

"I'm afraid you don't owe me any thanks.

Before that business out on the road, Nolan likely didn't have any opinion of you one way or the other. Now that you've refused to bow and scrape, he's your enemy. That's something I wouldn't wish on anyone."

"I'll learn to live with it," Matt said. "By the way, Mr. Gibson suggested that I come out and see where he found the hides. You and me both, that is, if you want to make the ride."

The sheriff thought about it a minute, and shook his head.

"It really isn't necessary. I'm satisfied that Ben was telling the truth, and looking at the hiding place wouldn't prove anything. Nolan could always say that Ben rigged things to prove his point." He looked at Matt thoughtfully, and added, "On the other hand, it wouldn't be a bad idea for you to go. You ought to get familiar with the layout around here, and this would be a good way to start. No telling when it could come in handy. Besides, I think you might enjoy visiting the Gibson ranch."

From the sheriff's expression, Matt deduced that he was making an oblique reference to Laura Gibson. He pretended to miss the point, and said innocently, "Yes, sir. Will tomorrow be all right?"

"Tomorrow will be fine," the sheriff said. "The next day we'd better stay in town, because Judge Jensen is due, and I may be able to talk him into a quick trial. I've got a bellyfull of our star boarder."

"Speaking of which," Matt said, lowering his voice, "the star boarder, as you call him, just offered me a thousand dollars, which I suppose was for letting him escape. I pretended to be interested, and before he was done, he practically admitted robbing that bank in New Mexico."

"Good. I was pretty sure already, and this cinches it. But don't mention his offer to the judge. It would only complicate things. Murder is a lot more serious crime than robbery."

"Yes, sir," Matt said. A disturbing possibility crossed his mind, and he asked casually, "How much territory does Judge Jensen cover?"

"Most of the eastern half of Arizona. Why? Do you think you might have run into him someplace?"

"No," Matt said, relieved that the judge had no official contact with Colorado. "I'm just interested in hearing about him. Is he well thought of?"

"Very," the sheriff said. "He's quite a character. About six feet four, with a small beard but no mustache. You've seen pictures of Abe Lincoln. That's as close as I can come to describing Judge Jensen. He sort of ambles when he walks, but his mind is going a mile a minute, as a lot of shyster lawyers have found out to their sorrow. You'll be able to form your own opinion in a couple of days."

The sheriff got up and went back toward the cell. He was smiling when he returned to the front of the room.

"Whatever you said back there seems to have at least one fortunate result. This is the longest our prisoner has gone without crabbing about something."

"He's probably busy figuring how he'll kill me

for fooling him," Matt said. "And for shooting his partner. Is there anything I'm supposed to be doing?"

The sheriff didn't answer until he had rolled a cigarette and lit it. Then he opened a drawer, took out a bunch of WANTED notices, and placed them on the desk.

"You might skim through these. This is an accumulation of about five years. Once in a while a picture is clear enough, or a description good enough, so that you could recognize the man if you saw him. Or woman. There's a couple of females in the batch. You can sit at the desk. I'm going over and talk to Doc Yarborough. I think my leg is enough better so that I can get rid of this blasted cane. If I did it without his permission, he'd be mad as a wet hen. See you later."

"Yes, sir," Matt said. He waited nervously for the sheriff to get out of sight, then bent over the stack of notices. A brief glance at the top one when the sheriff had laid them on the desk had made Matt's heart jump. A quick reading confirmed what he had suspected. It even gave his name, Matt Dixon. Of course there was no picture, but the description fitted him reasonably well. Or rather it fitted the way he had looked when he had left Gunnison. He hoped his changed appearance would keep him from being recognized. At any rate it had not betrayed him to the sheriff.

For a few minutes this was such a relief that Matt began to breathe easier. Then something brought him up short. Why had his notice been on top of the pack? Was it a trick to make him give himself away? He bolted out of the chair, reached the doorway in two quick strides, and peered out onto the street.

The sheriff was not in sight. Matt took his hand off his gun, and returned to the chair. After a bit he shook his head in self-reproach. Why *wouldn't* the notice be on top? If this stack was a five years' accumulation, as the sheriff had said, there probably wouldn't be more than an average of one or two a month. His had likely been the most recent, so it would naturally be on top. He had been stupid to suspect the sheriff of trickery. Somehow, this made him very glad.

The prisoner was yelling again, but Matt paid no attention. Should he leave the notice where it was, and take a chance on the sheriff's looking at it more closely and spotting the similarity between Matt and the man described? Or should he destroy it, while he had the chance, and shuffle the others around so that its absence wouldn't be noticed?

In the end he decided to leave the stack exactly as it had been given to him. He skimmed through the rest of the pile without recognizing any of the few blurred pictures, or the descriptions, which were so much alike that the words became meaningless. His mind wandered from what he was doing, and he thought about his father. Would there be a WANTED notice for him, filed away somewhere under an accumulation of dust and cobwebs? Probably not. They must have quit looking for him years ago. If anyone had ever really tried.

Funny, he hadn't thought much about his father lately. Finding him and killing him was the purpose of this search, but for the last few weeks more urgent matters had crowded it out of his mind. As soon as the Gunnison affair died down, he'd take up the quest again. Possibly the sheriff could have helped, but it was too late for that now. Two men looking for a father who had deserted his family would be too much of a coincidence to miss. The sheriff would catch on at once.

The prisoner hollered again, and this time Matt went back close enough to see him, while still staying out of reach. The prisoner was sitting on the edge of the bunk, his hands clasped across his belly. He was bent over so far that he had to look at Matt sideways.

"What's wrong?" Matt demanded.

"My guts are killing me," the prisoner groaned. "I think I've been poisoned."

"That's impossible. You had the same food we did." Yet despite his words, Matt was worried. What if the man was really sick? He debated with himself briefly, and decided on an experiment. He said unsympathetically, "What difference does it make, anyway. You might as well die now from a bellyache as in a couple of days at the end of a rope." He turned away.

"You son of a bitch!"

Matt whirled quickly and surprised the prisoner sitting up straight, no longer clutching his belly. He grinned.

"What happend to your gut-ache? Aren't you going to die after all?"

There was no answer, so Matt returned to the front. The sheriff was just coming in the door, a triumphant smile on his face.

"Look," he said, holding out his hands. "No cane. Doc Yarborough says I've improved enough to get along without it. If he hadn't, I was going to shove it down his throat. No, I take that back. The doctor's a good man. This town would be in a hell of a mess without him. Did anything happen while I was gone?"

"Well, our friend back there pretended to be sick, but he seems to have made a miraculous recovery. Oh, I looked through those notices. Like you said, they don't do much good. I think any one of the crooks they're looking for could walk in here right now and I wouldn't recognize him. Or her. How long do you have to keep them?"

"Supposedly until the wanted person either dies or is captured. Actually, about five years. Otherwise they'd clutter up the place. Why?"

"No special reason," Matt said. "I was just curious."

"Well, I'm more hungry than curious," the sheriff said. "How about it? Shall we go over to the cafe?"

"Suits me."

From the back of the room, the prisoner yelled, "What about me? I get hungry, too."

"Oh?" the sheriff said, winking at Matt. "Sick as you are, I didn't think you'd be interested in food. You probably shouldn't eat right now, anyway. Well, maybe a bowl of toast and warm milk wouldn't hurt you. I'll see what I can do."

To the accompaniment of the prisoner's curses, they left the office and crossed to the cafe.

Chapter Twelve

Matt was awakened during the night by what he at first took to be gunfire. Before he could get out of bed the sound was repeated, and he realized that it was only thunder. A brilliant flash which illuminated the room was followed so closely by another ear-shattering crash that he knew the lightning had struck nearby. He padded barefoot to the window and looked out.

There was no indication that the bolt had done any damage. None of the buildings in sight were ablaze, and no one was stirring. Apparently Holbrook's citizens were taking the electrical display in stride.

Matt had seen a good deal of lightning himself, especially in the Rockies, where he had derived a distinct thrill out of watching the jagged streaks bury themselves in the towering peaks, and listening to the thunder bounce from mountain to mountain. Here there were no mountains, but he was fascinated, and stood for some time watching the spectacle, while waiting for the rain to start.

Oddly enough, the rain didn't come. Instead, the lightning diminished in intensity as the storm moved east, to be succeeded by a strong wind, which set the hanging signs in front of several store buildings banging. The temperature dropped appreciably in a matter of minutes, and he was glad to get back into bed and pull the blanket up to his chin.

When morning came the wind was still blowing, but the sky was clear. From his window, Matt had an unobstructed view of the cafe, and he was pleased to see that smoke was already coming from the chimney, to be whipped away almost immediately by the wind. He splashed cold water on his face, dressed, and went downstairs and out of the hotel.

There was no one else abroad at this early hour. The street looked especially bare, since the wind had swept it clear of debris. Matt had to hang onto his hat to keep from losing it, and he sighed with relief when he had entered the cafe and forced the door shut behind him.

Ellen came out of the kitchen, smiled, and said with some surprise, "You fooled me. The sheriff is generally my first customer. Breakfast isn't ready yet. I don't generally open up until seven."

Matt glanced at the clock on the wall, whose hands pointed to six forty, and said apologetically, "I didn't realize it was so early. I don't mind waiting, though, if I won't be in the way."

"Of course you won't," Ellen said. "In fact if you want to come back in the kitchen, we can talk while I work. What did you think of the storm last night?"

"I liked it," Matt said, following her into the back room. "I always did get a kick out of lightning and thunder." He looked around the room, which was spotlessly clean, and sat down on a stool which Ellen indicated. "It surprised me, though, that there wasn't any rain. Where I grew up, the two always went together."

Ellen, who was at the stove, and had her back turned, said over her shoulder, "Where was that? I've never heard you mention where you came from."

The question was innocent enough, but it made Matt stiffen. No one, not even the sheriff, had asked him about his background. He hesitated so long that Ellen turned her head to look at him, then he said quickly, "The middle west. Ohio, to be specific."

"Oh?" Ellen said. "I've heard a lot about Ohio. My mother was born there. A little town named Pleasantville. Are you acquainted with the place?"

"No," Matt said. "I never had much to do with towns. I grew up on a farm." He braced himself for the next question, but it didn't materialize. Instead, Ellen changed the subject.

"I was born right here in Holbrook, and I've never been east of Arizona." She turned to face him, and added matter-of-factly, "My parents were on their way to California... of course that was before I was born... but my mother's health wasn't good, so when they got this far, they stopped. My mother died giving birth to me a few months later."

"I'm sorry."

"So am I," Ellen said. "It isn't easy for a man to bring up a child, especially a daughter. Of course Pa had a woman to help him for a while. She was Mexican. You've no doubt noticed that there are a lot of Mexicans in Holbrook. I'm sure she did her best; she even taught me her language, which has proved helpful. Still, it wasn't like having a real mother."

"Did your father start this restaurant?"

"No. He was a shoemaker by trade, and ran a saddle shop after coming west. He died when I was sixteen. By then I had a job in this restaurant. Years later, when the proprietor retired, I took over." She made a self deprecatory gesture. "You didn't ask for my life history; I hope I haven't bored you."

"I was interested in it," Matt said. "You seem to have done all right, even though you didn't have a mother."

"Well, I'm not the only woman to go through that unfortunate experience. In fact there's a similar situation right here. Laura Gibson, the girl you met after the funeral, was brought up by her father. Of course you know Ben Gibson. Ed. . . the sheriff, that is, told me about what happened yesterday out on the road. What do you think of the man? Ben Gibson, I mean. I can guess your opinion of Nolan."

"I like Mr. Gibson," Matt said sincerely. "Incidentally, I'll probably be seeing him again today. He invited me out to his place, and the sheriff thinks it's a good way for me to start getting acquainted with the territory."

"And with Laura Gibson?" Ellen suggested, laughing. "Well, the food's ready, if you are. I'll fix a plate for your prisoner, so you can take it over when you finish. Provided he isn't afraid of getting poisoned, that is."

Matt grinned, and left the kitchen. An hour later, after finishing breakfast, and delivering the prisoner's, which was received without thanks, and having ascertained from the sheriff that there was nothing for him to do in town, he was on his way to Double X.

The wind was still blowing, stirring up little dust-devils, which made Matt's horse skittish. It had erased the tracks where Gibson had turned his buggy the day before, but Matt thought he recognized the spot, and he looked off in the direction Nolan had ridden, which he presumed was toward Slash N. There was no one in sight, but he did see quite a few head of cattle, and in one instance came close enough to make out the Slash N brand on a steer's flank.

The turnoff to Double X was not hard to spot, and Matt swung his mount off the main road. Soon the ranch buildings came into sight: a one story adobe house, unpainted wooden barn with attached corral, and several smaller outbuildings. No one was in sight, but as Matt rode into the ranch yard proper, Laura Gibson stepped out of the barn, a shotgun cradled in her arm.

At least he assumed that it was Laura, although her garb of waist overalls, man's flannel shirt, and floppy-brimmed felt hat made her look quite different from the girl he had met in town.

The shotgun was a surprise, too, and worried him a little. Girls and guns were a dangerous combination. She might shoot him without meaning to. For the sake of his own safety, he reined his horse to a stop, held his hands shoulder high, and called, "Be careful where you point that scattergun, Miss.

It might go off. I'm Martin Davis, Sheriff Durham's deputy."

"I can see you. . . now," Laura said, lowering the shotgun. "But from a distance I didn't recognize you. And don't worry about the gun going off. It won't until I want it to."

Matt rode closer then, touched the brim of his hat, and said, "I'm sorry if I startled you. Your pa invited me to come out. He was going to show me where he found those calf hides."

"I know," Laura said, but she didn't smile. Matt wondered why. She had been pleasant enough in town. The look she gave him now might indicate either annoyance or embarrassment, and he couldn't account for either reaction. However, she said politely enough, "Pa isn't here. It's too bad you made the ride for nothing."

It was obviously Matt's cue to leave, but he didn't intend to be dismissed so casually. Instead of riding away, he stepped out of the saddle and said, "I'm in no big rush, so I'll wait. How soon do you expect him back?"

She seemed a little disconcerted, which was hard to understand.

"I really don't know, Mr. Davis. Maybe within an hour, maybe not till sundown." She hesitated, then added, "I was about to have a bite to eat. You're welcome to join me if you want to."

"Thanks," Matt said. "But you don't have to call me 'mister.' Just Martin is good enough. May I put my horse in the barn?"

"Of course. Then come to the house. I'll go ahead and put the coffee on."

Matt nodded, and led his horse into the barn,

where it seemed unnaturally quiet after having listened to the wind all morning. He put his horse in the first empty stall, noting wiht approval that everything was in good order. After exchanging the horse's bridle for a halter, he started to take off the saddle, but thought better of it and merely loosened the cinch. It wouldn't be advisable to give the impression that he intended to stay over-long.

There was a wash bench with a basin outside the kitchen door. Matt stopped to wash his hands, wiped them on his pants because he couldn't see any towel, and entered the house.

As he had expected, he was in the kitchen. Front doors were used for formal occasions, not for unexpected visitors. He had time for a quick glance around the room, noting that it, like the barn, was well kept, and then Laura came through a doorway. She had removed the floppy hat, and had evidently taken time to brush her hair, which was soft and glossy, the way it had been the day of the funeral. Glossy, at any rate; he had an almost uncontrollable urge to touch it and see if it felt as soft as it looked.

"What are you staring at?" Laura demanded.

"Staring? I didn't mean. . . " Matt felt the red creeping into his face.

Well, at any rate it had made Laura smile for the first time, and he didn't try to finish the sentence.

"Sit down," Laura said. "The coffee isn't quite ready. I hope you don't mind cold food. So long as it isn't Nolan's veal, that is."

Matt grinned.

"Your pa sure out-foxed Nolan on that one, didn't he? You should have been there to see

Nolan's face."

"I wish I had," Laura said, smiling. "No, I guess it's just as well I wasn't. I might have told Nolan what I think of him." She looked at Matt appraisingly. "Pa tells me that's what *you* did, but in a polite way. I think the coffee is hot by now."

Matt watched her fill two cups and place them on the table. She got a chunk of cold roast beef out of a cooler, cut several thick slices of bread, and handed Matt the knife.

"You can help yourself to the meat. You know your capacity better than I do."

Matt cut off a reasonable portion, put it between two slices of bread, and started eating. Laura did the same, and for a few minutes there was no conversation. Matt finished first, sipped coffee while Laura caught up with him, then said, "Something's been puzzling me. Do you always greet visitors with a shotgun?"

Laura shook her head.

"Not in the past, but I can't make any promises about the future. How much do you know about Nolan?"

"Only what the sheriff has told me. And of course what I saw for myself yesterday. Why? Did you think I might be one of his men when I rode in?"

"I couldn't be sure," Laura said. "And I wasn't taking any chances. Did the sheriff tell you how Nolan crowded out over half of the small ranchers?"

"He mentioned it," Matt acknowledged. "And so did your pa, out on the road yesterday. Do you really think Nolan means to take over this one?"

"Yes," Laura said unhesitatingly. "This and all the others. Unless. . . "

"Unless what?"

"Nothing," Laura said. "More coffee?"

"No, thank you," Matt said. He was wondering what she had been about to say. He couldn't help thinking it might have something to do with her father's absence. Ben Gibson didn't strike him as the kind of rancher to leave everything in charge of a girl. Not unless he had a compelling reason. It was something Matt wanted to discuss with the sheriff. He pushed back his chair and stood up.

"I'm obliged to you for the meal. I guess I won't wait for your pa after all, since you don't know when he'll be back."

"That's up to you," Laura said, but she sounded relieved. "Before you leave, though, there's one thing I'd like to get straight. Shall we go outside?"

Wondering what she was up to, Matt followed her out. She reached into a trash barrel beside the door, extracted an empty tomato can, and walked in the opposite direction from the barn. When they had gone about fifty yards, she turned and held out her hand.

"May I borrow your revolver, please?"

Still in the dark, Matt handed her his sixgun. He couldn't resist saying, "Be careful. It's loaded."

"Really?" she said innocently. She handed him the tin can. "Do me another favor. Throw this as far as you can."

Beginning to get an inkling of what she was up to, Matt threw the can. It rolled to a stop some twenty or thirty yards away. While he was still watching it, the gun roared, and the tomato can took a crazy hop. In rapid succession, Laura fired four more shots, each one sending the can a bit farther on its way. She turned to Matt and extended the pistol butt first.

"I presume, Mr. Davis, that you always leave one chamber empty?"

Matt nodded mutely, and Laura said, "I also presume that in the future you won't take it for granted that a woman can't handle a gun without shooting somebody." She grinned. "Did I surprise you, Mr. Davis?"

Matt nodded again, but he wasn't thinking too much about her dexterity with a gun. Looking at her this way, with the wind blowing her hair, and her eyes sparkling with triumph, did something to him. Without stopping to consider the consequences, he put his arms around her, pulled her close, and kissed her on the lips.

For a second she seemed to respond, or was it wishful thinking? The she broke loose, backed off a step, and stared at him round-eyed.

"What in the world was that for, Mr. Davis?"

She didn't seem too angry, and Matt grinned.

"Turn about is fair play. You surprised me with your shooting. Now we're even. Tell your pa I'll talk to him later."

Without waiting for a reply, he turned and walked to the barn. When he rode out a few minutes later she wasn't in sight. But he could still taste the sweetness of her lips.

Chapter Thirteen

Nolan, seething at the failure of his plan to implicate Ben Gibson in cattle stealing, and further enraged over the way in which the new deputy had stood up to him, had returned to the Slash N headquarters, handed his reins to one of his men, Nate Isaacs, who was making some repairs to the corral, and stalked toward the house. Isaacs, the oldest man on the crew, had very wisely held his silence. He kept out of Nolan's way insofar as possible, even when the latter was in a good mood, for he was well aware that his age, and the fact that he was beginning to slow down, made his job precarious. Judging from the look on Nolan's face right now, it would take very little to make him explode.

Actually, Nolan was hardly aware of Isaacs as an individual. There was no rapport between himself and his men. None of them except his ramrod, Dyke Blodgett, and Dakota Groves, his *de facto* bodyguard, ever entered the house. Blodgett, all of whose thirty years had been spent on ranches, was a capable foreman, and as such was responsible for the day-to-day operation of the ranch, which left Nolan free to devote most of his time to various devious plans. Blodgett carried out Nolan's orders to the letter, even though this sometimes went against his grain. Unlike most of the crew, whose only allegiance was to the high wages which Nolan paid, Blodgett lived by the old maxim that a man was loyal to the brand for which he worked, in his case Slash N.

Nolan turned just before entering the house, and called peremptorily to Isaacs, "When Groves comes in, tell him I want to see him."

Isaacs nodded, waited for Nolan to go into the house and slam the door, then led the horse to the barn and started unsaddling. He wondered what had put Nolan in such an ugly frame of mind. Probably he would never know, but of one thing he was sure; it was going to mean trouble for somebody. And Isaacs didn't like trouble. For the hundredth time, he thought about quitting, and as usual, he abandoned the idea. If he could get another job, which was extremely doubtful, it would have to be with one of the small ranchers, and he had the feeling that this would land him in more trouble than ever. At his age, he didn't relish the idea of going elsewhere to make a fresh start. He'd just hang on, try to keep out of Nolan's sight, and hope for the best.

Inside the house, Nolan went directly to his desk, took a bottle and a tumbler out of a drawer, and poured himself a healthy slug of whiskey, which he downed without stopping for breath. Although he was not normally a heavy drinker, he refilled the glass and began pacing up and down the big room, kicking aside objects in his path, and sloshing liquor on the floor. Dama Gibson! Why the hell did he have to find those hides? And ~~double damn~~ that deputy! It was aggravating enough having to deal with a sheriff who refused to knuckle under. For an upstart deputy to act so independently was too much. By God, he'd put an end to that!

Gradually, as Nolan's anger slackened, he began to think more clearly. Gibson and the deputy would have to pay, of course, but there was a third culprit, the man who had let himself be seen by Gibson's daughter. Dakota Groves? It didn't seem likely. Groves was too smart to pull a stunt like that. Or was he?

After finishing his second drink, Nolan was calm enough to sit down at his desk. He re-corked the whiskey bottle, put it and the glass back in a drawer, and opened another drawer, from which he took a rolled sheet of paper. With a sweep of his arm he cleared a space on the desk top, then flattened the paper, and put weights on the corners to hold it down.

Unrolled, the paper became a map, its boundaries enclosing an area some fifty miles square, of which Slash N was the approximate center. The town of Holbrook was indicated by an inked-in circle with the abbreviation "Holb." There was nothing to show the extent of Nolan's property, but each of the other ranches had been drawn in, apparently to scale. Several of these were cross-hatched, and anyone familiar with the region would recognize them as the small outfits which had been taken over by Nolan. The remaining six bore the names Gibson, Jennings, Nordquest, Otis, Debrow, and Schloemp.

The map never failed to lift Nolan's spirits, and

once again the charm worked. In his mind's eye he could see the rest of the ranches blocked out, leaving Slash N in possession of the whole range. Once that happened, the name Nolan would be right up there alongside those of Goodnight, Loving, and others who had started small, but who, by using running irons, swinging a wide loop, and in other ways bending a few laws, had become rich and famous. And who could say that there wouldn't be a title in front of it? Governor Nolan? Senator Nolan? He rolled the words over his tongue, and liked the taste.

There would be other changes, too. Take this house, for instance. It would be refurbished with fancy new furniture freighted in from Kansas City or St. Louis, and staffed with servants. And of course there would be a woman to give orders to the servants, and to preside over the stylish dinners and parties which would be given for the men he wanted to impress. Not just any woman. . . Ellen Troup. She had been playing hard to get, but she was too smart to turn down a proposition such as this. Especially after the sheriff had been taken out of circulation, which he surely would be.

This brought Nolan back to that aggravating incident out on the road. The deputy must be made to pay for his insolence, too. And of course Ben Gibson, but that was part of a bigger plan.

The room was getting dark, and Nolan was surprised to discover that he had been fantasizing for several hours. He also realized that he was hungry. He re-rolled the map, put it back in the drawer, and was about to go out to the kitchen and tell Lew Wong to prepare his supper, when there was a knock at the door, and Dakota Groves called, "Is it all right to come in, boss?"

"The door's unlocked," Nolan replied, and settled back in his chair.

Groves opened the door and came in. If he noticed that things had been disturbed, he kept it to himself.

"Nate Isaacs said you wanted to see me."

"That's right," Nolan acknowledged. It didn't occur to him to invite Groves to sit down, nor did Groves expect it. Groves listened silently as Nolan recounted his visit to the sheriff's office, and the subsequent events. Telling about it rekindled some of Nolan's anger, and he finished by saying bluntly, "It would have worked except for that girl seeing somebody on the road and making Gibson suspicious. Do you have any idea who the man might have been?"

"No," Groves said. "Except that it wasn't me. I came straight back to the ranch after burying the hides."

Nolan didn't know whether or not to believe this, but he had no intention of calling Groves a liar, so he simply said, "Chances are it was a stranger, but if it wasn't, if it was someone from here, I want to know about it. See what you can find out."

"I'll nose around a little," Groves said. "But about this new deputy. You ain't going to let him get away with it, are you? If you do, he'll be bragging all over town. Say the word, and I'll take care of it. I know ways to make a man go for his gun."

"I'm sure you do," Nolan said. "But I don't

want anyone from here getting involved. Besides, I have a better idea. You know, of course, that the sheriff has a man in jail, waiting to be tried for killing Al Gregg."

Dakota Groves's expression didn't change, but his nod was enough to make Nolan continue.

"That prisoner, I don't know what his name is, must hate that new deputy's guts, being as it was the deputy who held a gun on him until the sheriff arrived, not to mention killing the fellow's partner."

"I reckon so," Groves said. "But I don't. . ."

Nolan went on as though there had been no interruption.

"If the prisoner should happen to get his hands on a pistol, say maybe tomorrow night. . . well, do you get the idea?"

"Sure, boss," Groves said, his expression showing comprehension. "Is there anything else?"

"That's all," Nolan said, and watched Groves leave the room before getting up to go to the kitchen.

Out in the yard, Groves smothered a grin. Nolan must suspect him of having been the man who had been seen by Gibson's daughter, and of course he was right, but he had been afraid to come out in the open and say so. It was a nice feeling, knowing that you were working for a man who was afraid of you. All you had to do was play your cards right, and you could end up a wealthy man. Especially if Nolan became as rich and powerful as he intended to, and Groves didn't doubt for a minute that he would.

Satisfied with the way things were going, Groves

crossed to the cookshack, where he conveniently forgot to bring up the subject of the man who had been seen on the road. He didn't, however, forget about Gibson's girl. It had been a mistake letting her see him, but fortunately he had controlled himself before any harm had been done. The next time they met, it would be under different circumstances. He wanted her, and what he wanted, he usually got.

Chapter Fourteen

When Matt got back to town, he stopped at the livery stable. Moose Dreyfuss, the blacksmith who had fitted new shoes to Matt's horse, was working at the forge. The reason for his nickname was obvious. He was well over six feet tall, had shoulders roughly a yard wide, and the bulging muscles associated with his trade. Like so many men with these physical qualifications, he had a mild disposition, and a soft voice. Without waiting to be asked, he left his work and came over to lift the hoof which had been injured.

On completing his inspection, he nodded with approval, looked up, and said, "Seems to be doing all right. You were smart not to ride him after he began to limp."

"Not smart," Matt said. "Just careful. He's carried me a long way, and I hope he'll go a lot farther before being put out to pasture."

"Does that mean you're already thinking about leaving?"

"Not right away. But I don't intend to stay here forever. Not that I don't like the place. Holbrook is a good town for someone who's ready to settle down. I haven't reached that point yet."

"No, I suppose not," Moose said. "But if you

had, you couldn't find a better man to work for than Sheriff Durham."

"I agree with you on that," Matt said. "Well, thanks for doing such a good job on my horse. By the way, I won't be stabling him in the livery barn any more. The sheriff has an extra stall he says I can use. I've already told Mr. Boggs."

The sheriff was at his desk, and looked up when Matt came in.

"How're things out at Double X? Did Ben show you where he found the hides?"

"He wasn't there," Matt said, and the sheriff looked surprised.

"Oh? Did Laura tell you where he'd gone?"

"No. She didn't seem to know when he'd be back, either. Maybe I'm imagining things, but it struck me that she didn't want to talk about it."

"That's odd," the sheriff mused. He started to add something, then apparently remembered about the prisoner, and changed it to, "Laura didn't run you off, did she?"

Matt shook his head.

"She wasn't exactly tickled to see me, but after she made sure who I was, she put down her shotgun and invited me to share her noon meal." He grinned. "After which she gave me a lesson in pistol shooting. With my own gun, at that. If there's ever a war, I hope she's on my side."

The sheriff's grin matched Matt's.

"I could've warned you, but I didn't want to spoil the fun.". His grin faded, and he added curiously, "You say she was toting a shotgun?"

When Matt nodded, the sheriff got up and motioned toward the door. "Come out front a minute. There's something I want to show you."

128

"Yes, sir," Matt said, and followed him out onto the sidewalk. The sheriff moved several paces from the doorway, and glanced both ways along the street to make sure they wouldn't be overheard.

"I didn't want to talk where the prisoner could hear us. Not that I expect him to be around long enough to do any harm, but there's no sense taking a chance. What you said about Gibson being absent on some mission that Laura didn't want to talk about, plus the fact that she was lugging a shotgun, worries me. It isn't like Ben to leave the ranch, not when there's just the two of them to run it, and if he'd just been out moving cattle or something, Laura would have told you. All the times I've ridden out there, nobody ever met me with a shotgun. That, along with what happened yesterday between Ben and Nolan, makes me wonder if there isn't trouble afoot."

"Do you think Mr. Gibson might be doing something to get even?"

"No. He isn't so foolish as to buck an outfit like Slash N single-handed. For that matter, he isn't foolish at all. He's smart enough to realize that Nolan isn't going to let up on him, just because that stunt with the calf hides backfired."

"So?" Matt prompted, not sure what the sheriff was driving at.

"So he may be talking to the owners of the other small ranches, trying to sell them the idea that they've got to band together for self protection." He shook his head. "Dammit, I've been expecting this for a long time, and trying to make myself believe it wouldn't happen. Not that I blame Gibson. In his place, I'd likely feel the way he does. But they don't stand a chance, six little ranches scattered all over, against a big one like Slash N, with a crew made up mostly of gunslingers who'll do anything Nolan tells them to."

"Isn't there anything the law can do about it?" Matt asked.

"Not a damned thing," the sheriff said. "Oh, I'll try to talk some sense into Gibson and the others, but there's no law against forming some kind of association, or whatever they choose to call it. And if there's trouble, Nolan will manage somehow to make it look like the other side started it. God! I hate to think what it will be like around here if a shooting war breaks out."

Matt thought about Laura, and his lips tightened. He could picture what might happen to her if Nolan turned loose his men.

Apparently his expression gave some indication of what he was thinking, for the sheriff said reassuringly, "Nothing's liable to happen right away. If I know ranchers, and I think I do, they'll do a lot of backing and filling before they get organized. In the meantime, we've got other business to attend to. Judge Jensen is due before the day's over, and I'm hoping he'll try our prisoner tomorrow. The judge doesn't generally hold court on Saturday, but in this case he might make an exception. Now if you'll stick around and keep an eye on things, I'm going to throw a saddle on my horse and take a little ride. I'm anxious to see if my bum leg can take it. Don't tell Doc Yarborough!"

Matt wanted to remonstrate, but he was sure the sheriff wouldn't be dissuaded, so he merely nodded and went into the office. A glance toward the back of the room showed him that the prisoner was

130

standing on his bunk, peering out through the iron-barred window. Matt felt a fleeting sympathy for the man, and had to remind himself that he was a cold blooded murderer as well as a thief. No telling how many innocent men he had killed in addition to Matt's predecessor. And of course he would just as readily kill Matt if given the opportunity. Or anyone else who got in his way. The sheriff was right. A prompt trial was in order, followed by a quick hanging.

Returning to the doorway, Matt looked out at the street. The sheriff was not in sight, apparently having stayed off the main street so as not to be seen by Doc Yarborough. A few townsfolk were going about their business, two women talking in front of the mercantile, the saddlemaker perched precariously on an empty box as he replaced his sign, which had been torn loose by last night's wind. Matt wondered idly if it was the shop which had been run by Ellen Troup's father.

Thinking of Ellen brought to mind Laura Gibson. He could still see the surprised look on her face when he had kissed her. Well, she couldn't have been any more surprised than he was. He didn't ordinarily act so impulsively. Of course Laura was no ordinary girl. She wasn't the first girl he had kissed, but this was different.

Just thinking about it brought a smile to his lips. Then he remembered what the sheriff had said about the possibility of a war between Nolan and the other ranchers, and the smile vanished. If trouble were to break out, Laura would be in the thick of it. Grim faced, he went into the office, sat down at the sheriff's desk, and began flipping through the WANTED posters without actually focusing on them.

The sheriff, as Matt had guessed, had taken a back road which hit the main highway a mile north of town. Getting into the saddle had been painful, since it had necessitated putting most of his weight on his left leg, but he was gratified to find that the actual riding didn't cause excessive discomfort, even when he let the horse gallop, which it was eager to do, after having been idle so long.

Like Matt, the sheriff soon began thinking about the danger of a showdown between Nolan on one side, and Ben Gibson and the rest of the small ranchers on the other. The odds against such an uneven match-up ending in favor of the small ranchers were about ten to one. Ben Gibson must realize this, for he was an intelligent man, yet he would probably go ahead anyhow.

In a way, the sheriff couldn't blame him. Forced to choose between knuckling under or putting up a fight, a man like Gibson was certain to choose the latter. And having once made his choice, he wouldn't back down, even though it meant risking his ranch, his life, and, what he would consider more important, the safety of his daughter whom he loved so dearly.

The sheriff wasn't as sure of the other ranchers. Even if Gibson convinced them that they had to join forces against Nolan, some of them might falter when blood began to flow. None of them were cowards, not Lew Jennings, Nordquest, Dutch Schloemp, Will Otis, nor Hank Debrow. They had all faced danger many times: blizzards, stampedes, wild mustangs. At least two of them, Jennings and Nordquest, had been around when there was still Indian trouble. They would risk death defending their homes or families from impending danger, but a deal like this. . .

The sheriff swore silently. ~~he can tell~~ to see something like this coming, and not be able to stop it. But what could he do? Nolan hadn't openly broken any laws. Of course there were those two stubborn ranchers who had died as the result of mysterious "accidents," but there had been no evidence to back up the general suspicion that Nolan had been involved. And even if there *were* tangible proof that he was guilty, what could one man, even though he wore a sheriff's star, do about it? Or a sheriff and one deputy? It would take a troop of cavalry to bring Nolan to jail. Or a large posse, which in this case was out of the question.

The sheriff's gloomy thoughts were interrupted by the appearance of a buggy which, as it drew near, he recognized as that of Judge Jensen. He reined up, waited for the rig to pull alongside, and leaned down to shake hands with the driver, who, as he had so often noticed, resembled Abe Lincoln.

"Welcome back, Judge. Did you have a satisfactory trip?"

"Thanks, Sheriff," Judge Jensen said, his handclasp firm. "A busy one, anyway. Two killers sentenced to hang, a wife beater shipped off to Yuma, plus several odds and ends, including a couple of not guilty verdicts. Anything new in Holbrook?"

"You aren't going to like this," the sheriff warned. "But there's more work waiting for you here. Some drifter killed my deputy, Al Gregg. He did it in front of half a dozen reliable witnesses, who all agree that the killing was unprovoked. I've got the killer in jail, and I hope you'll break one of your rules by trying him tomorrow, even though it's a Saturday."

"Oh Lord! I was looking forward to going fishing. Do you really want the trial so soon?"

"I'd appreciate it."

"Very well, the fish will have to wait," Judge Jensen said resignedly. "Any other bad news?"

"No," the sheriff told him. "The rest of it is good. I already have a new deputy, a young man by the name of Martin Davis. He was innocently involved in the affair in which Al Gregg was killed. I'll tell you about it later. The other thing is that my leg is almost well."

"Glad to hear it," the judge said. "Well, I'll see you in court tomorrow. Make it ten o'clock. I'm at least going to have the luxury of sleeping late for a change."

At midnight, the prisoner was lying awake, staring at the small square of light which marked the window of his cell. Despite his tough, defiant attitude, he was innately a coward, terrified at the thought of dying. Until now, he hadn't worried too much about it, for he had committed many crimes without beng punished, and had fully expected his luck to hold. This confidence had shrunk abruptly when the sheriff had informed him that the judge was in town, and would hold his trial tomorrow.

He had already tried every trick he knew to make his escape, first by attempting to bribe that damned deputy with the promise of money, feigning sickness, trying to loosen the bars in his cell window, and always alert for a chance to catch the sheriff off guard on one of his trips to the privy out back. The deputy had refused to be bribed or tricked, the bars were secure, and the sheriff had kept far enough away so that there had been no chance to jump him before he could shoot.

Now there were only a few hours left, and he had run out of ideas. Of course there was one chance in a hundred that he would be found innocent. About as much likelihood as that the cell door would miraculously unlock itself!

At this point in his thinking, his ears caught the rustle of stealthy footsteps outside, followed by the faint clink of metal against metal. He waited tensely for something else to happen, but all he heard was the footsteps receding, and then silence. Completely mystified, he stood up on the bunk. His eyes caught the glint of starlight on metal, and his groping fingers closed on what he immediatly recognized by feel as a revolver.

Dumbfounded, he sat down on the edge of the bunk and ran his hands over the pistol. It was small, compared to the one he usually carried, but he knew it could be deadly at short range. His exploring fingers ascertained that all of the chambers were loaded.

Another man might have speculated on who had brought about this minor miracle, but the prisoner, his confidence restored, simply took it as proof that his luck was still running good. Instead of wasting time trying to figure out what had happened, he began planning how best to take advantage of it.

The obvious answer, of course, was to wait until only one of his jailers was present, get the drop on him, and make him unlock the cell door. This had several disadvantages. In the first place, he was afraid that the sheriff, or the deputy, for that matter, would risk being shot rather than release a prisoner. Also, even though he waited until only one of them was in the office, he couldn't be sure that the other one wouldn't return at the critical moment. And there was also the matter of a quick getaway. From his cell he couldn't see the street, so he wouldn't know whether there was a horse readily available.

After much thought, he arrived at what he considered an almost perfect solution. He would conceal the gun inside his waistband, underneath his shirt. The small size of the gun made this easy. Let them hold their trial. If by some remote chance it went in his favor, which could conceivably happen, for instance if the judge was drunk, he would walk out a free man. If, as he fully expected, the judge found him guilty, there would still be time to use the gun. And his escape would be made simpler because the street was sure to be thronged with folks who had come to town for the trial, as well as ranchers in Holbrook for their Saturday shopping.

The more he thought about it, the better he liked it. He would have his pick of horses. And, best of all, the sheriff wouldn't dare shoot at him for fear of hitting an innocent bystander. As for the deputy, he wouldn't be in condition to make trouble, since the first bullet in the mysteriously delivered gun had his name on it. He had it coming for sticking his damned nose into that business at the saloon.

Satisfied with his plan, the prisoner lay down and was soon asleep.

Chapter Fifteen

Sleep didn't come as quickly to the sheriff. For one thing, his leg was painful, presumably as the result of his ride. This didn't really worry him, since it had hurt ten times as badly the first few days after he had been shot, and he was resigned to a lengthy period of recovery before it was completely well.

There were other, more important reasons for his inability to sleep. One of these was the upcoming trial. So far as he knew, it would be routine, and quickly disposed of. Of course the prisoner could conceivably prolong things by demanding a jury, but this seemed unlikely, since he must know that public sentiment in Holbrook would be against him, and that he would stand a better chance if his fate were in the hands of an impartial judge. But a man whose life was at stake was bound to be desperate, and would try anything to avoid the noose. It was even remotely possible that he had unknown allies who would try to spring him free.

There was an even more disturbing problem, the possibility, no, *probability*, of trouble between Nolan and the small ranchers. Every lawman the sheriff had ever talked with dreaded getting involved in a range war, and he was no exception. It would be bad enough if the antagonists were strangers; it was twice as hard when some of them were your friends. Even the best of men are prone to act out of character in the heat of battle. Ben Gibson, for all that he was by nature a peaceful, law-abiding citizen, might, if crowded into a corner, step beyond the pale of the law, might even be deliberately goaded into it by some action on the part of Nolan. The idea of having to arrest Gibson was repugnant. At times like this, the sheriff felt like turning in his badge.

Then there was Matt, or Martin, as he now called himself. In the few days since Matt's arrival at Holbrook, the sheriff had developed a genuine liking for him. It had nothing to do with Matt's being his son. He would have felt the same way toward anyone with Matt's attributes. It was hard to believe that such a person could be guilty of the crimes with which he was charged. Just as it was hard for the sheriff to believe that he, himself, had once run off and deserted his family. Or that he was harboring a man wanted by the law.

Sooner or later the truth was bound to come out. Someone, perhaps a bounty hunter, would see through Matt's disguise, and try to take him in. Or Matt would find out that the sheriff was his father, whom he had vowed to kill. Would he go through with the threat, and thus become the murderer they claimed he was?

It was long past midnight when the sheriff fell into a fitful sleep. He awoke at daylight, groggy, and with none of his problems solved. He forced himself to get up and go through the customary morning ritual, then went to the cafe.

Ellen greeted him cheerfully, but there was concern in her eyes, and in her voice as she asked, "Is something wrong, Ed? Something you haven't told me about?"

"You know we don't have any secrets," the sheriff said, attempting a smile. "No, there's nothing new. If I look uglier than usual, it's because I spent most of the night trying to figure things out, when I should have been sleeping."

"Isn't there anything I can do to help?"

"I'm afraid not," the sheriff said. Then he grinned, and changed it to, "Well, there's one thing. You can bring me some breakfast. Maybe after I've eaten I'll be fit to associate with."

Before Ellen could answer, the door was opened, and Matt entered the cafe. Ellen welcomed him with a smile, to which he responded by taking off his hat and saying, "Good morning, Miss Troup," after which Ellen returned to the kitchen. She hadn't bothered to take his order, since she was sure he would want a duplicate of the sheriff's meal. After that first day, he had even asked for his eggs straight up, instead of scrambled. She wondered if his taste had changed, or if he was subconsciously trying to emulate the sheriff.

In the cafe proper, Matt as usual took a stool one position away from the sheriff, who asked him curiously, "How come you always say 'Miss Troup,' when everyone else calls her Ellen?"

"I don't rightly know," Matt said, and then, after giving it a moment's thought, "I suppose it's the way I was brought up. My mother was pretty much of a stickler about things like that."

"I know," the sheriff said, without thinking, and then, at Matt's puzzled look, "What I mean is, my mother was the same way."

Apparently this satisfied Matt, for he said, "I stuck my head in the office on the way over. Our lodger is sound asleep. I don't see how he can do it, knowing as he must that before the day is over he may be sentenced to hang. If it was me, I'd be pacing the floor."

"Maybe he knows something we don't," the sheriff said, frowning.

"Like what?"

"I don't know, but it bothers me. I'll be glad when the trial's over. Until it is, we're going to have to be extra careful."

Rex Bates, the banker, chose that moment to enter the cafe. He was a rather prim little man who seldom smiled. Seldom showed any emotion, for that matter, except on that one occasion when he thought his bank had been robbed. He said a polite, "Good morning," and added, "I understand Judge Jensen intends to hold court today. I suppose it will be in the school house?"

"That's right," the sheriff said. "Ten o'clock. Do you plan on attending?"

"No," Bates said. "I can't leave the bank. But I imagine you'll have a crowd. Somehow or other everybody seems to find out when anything special is going to happen."

The sheriff nodded, and Bates turned away to sit down at one of the tables. His presence put a damper on further conversation, so Matt and the sheriff exchanged only small talk as they ate the breakfasts which Ellen placed before them. After waiting on the banker, Ellen brought an extra plate of food. The sheriff looked at it, and said wryly, "Well, if he finishes all this, we can say the condemned man ate a hearty meal. Only maybe I'm getting ahead of myself. He hasn't been condemned yet. I still have the feeling that something may go wrong."

"It won't," Ellen promised. "But anyway, good luck."

"Thanks," the sheriff said, and picked up the extra plate. He and Matt left the cafe.

It was only a little past seven, but a few early comers had already ridden or driven into town. The sheriff looked them over carefully, and was relieved that the faces were all familiar. Of course if the prisoner had friends who planned to interfere, they would keep out of sight until the crucial moment.

The prisoner was awake, and seemed less tense than the sheriff felt. He grinned, and said mockingly, "I reckon this is the last breakfast you'll have to bring me. I'm going to miss the free grub." He winked, and added, "Don't look so glum; I'll still be eating regular."

"You sound pretty sure of yourself," the sheriff said.

"Why not? That Judge Jensen you've been telling me about must be a smart hombre. He ain't going to find me guilty after I explain that all I did was defend myself." With this he sat on the edge of the bunk and began to eat. He certainly didn't act like a man whose hours were numbered. The sheriff frowned at him a moment, then turned away to speak to Matt.

"I'm going over to the schoolhouse and get things set up. You'd better stick around here, just in case."

By ten o'clock, when Judge Jensen entered the schoolhouse, the place was packed. Some of the luckier spectators were seated at the pupils' desks, but the majority were standing around the sides of the room, or perched precariously on window sills. The teacher's desk would serve as a judge's bench, and a chair had been placed alongside it for the use of witnesses. There was also a makeshift bench in front of the permanent desks, and this was occupied by the sheriff and his prisoner, who was not handcuffed. In anticipation of this close proximity, the sheriff had given his gun to Matt, who was stationed near the doorway. A gun would be of no use to the sheriff in this crowded room, and might prove too much of a temptation to the prisoner. Since all the spectators had been forced to surrender their pistols before entering the building, Matt's was presumably the only weapon in the room.

The judge's arrival silenced the murmur of the crowd, for he was an impressive individual, towering above everybody else in the place. Evn though he was not wearing judicial robes, he had the look of a judge. Without glancing right or left, he strode to the front of the room, sat down at the teacher's desk, took a gavel out of his pocket, waited a few seconds for absolute silence, then banged the gavel and said, "The Third Circuit Court of the Territory of Arizona is now in session. Judge Jensen presiding."

In a more formal setting, this might have

sounded odd, since he was in effect taking over the duties of bailiff and clerk in addition to his own, but nobody here seemed to notice. After a deliberate visual survey of the room, he said, "The first case on today's docket is that of the Territory of Arizona versus John Doe. Is the accused present?"

"Yes, Your Honor," the sheriff said, rising to his feet. When the prisoner remained seated, he bent down and said in an undertone, "Stand up, ~~damn it!~~"

John Doe, as the judge had christened him, took his time about rising, after which he grinned impudently at the judge.

"This is all a big mistake, mister. I was just. . ."

The gavel cut him short.

"Not now, Mr. Doe. You'll have a chance to testify. By the way, would you prefer to be called by your right name?"

"John Doe's good enough for me, mister."

"Very well. However, I prefer to be addressed as 'Your Honor.' Please bear that in mind."

"Sure, mister. . . I mean, Your Honor."

"Good. Before you sit down, are you represented by counsel?" At the prisoner's confused expression, he amended this to, "Do you have a lawyer?"

"What the. . . what do I want with a lawyer? I ain't done. . ."

Again the gavel silenced him.

"You may sit down, Mr. Doe."

Looking at the prisoner, the sheriff had the uncomfortable feeling that something was wrong. The man didn't strike him as being brave, but he didn't act like someone facing an almost certain death sentence.

Judge Jensen had taken a sheet of paper out of his pocket and was reading it. When he finished, he said evenly, "According to the complaint, the prisoner is accused of having without provocation shot and killed one Al Gregg, a deputy sheriff. In cases involving a charge of this nature, the accused is entitled to trial by jury. Mr. Doe, what is your wish in this matter?"

The prisoner scowled as though in deep thought, then asked suspiciously, "Supposing I don't want a jury? Then what happens?"

"In that case, I, as the presiding judge, will render the verdict. In other words, I will decide whether you are guilty or innocent."

The prisoner turned to look at the spectators, apparently didn't like what he saw, and said harshly, "I reckon I'll take a chance on you, mister . . . I mean Your Honor."

A faint smile touched the judge's lips, but he said soberly, "Very well. In the absence of a prosecuting attorney, I will take it upon myself to call the witnesses. Will Mr. Bart Holmgren please take the stand."

Holmgren, who had apparently expected to be called, was near the front of the room. He took the oath, then sat down in the witness chair and looked inquiringly at the judge, who said formally, "Please state your name and occupation."

"Bart Holmgren. I'm bartender at the saloon."

"And were you present at the time of the alleged shooting?"

"Yes, sir, I mean yes, Your Honor."

"Then suppose you tell us, in your own words, what happened."

"Sure, Judge. This feller here..." he pointed at the prisoner, "and another jasper I don't know, was drinkin' at the bar when Al Gregg came in. They didn't like something he said, and..."

"Just a minute," the judge interrupted. "Do you happen to know what it was that he said?"

"Yes, sir, he asked them if they was only passing through, or if they was planning to stay a while."

"You may continue."

"Well, they didn't seem to like it. I guess they..."

"Please confine yourself to the facts, Mr. Holmgren. No guessing."

"Okay," Holmgren said. "Anyway, one thing led to another, until this feller here..." again pointing at the prisoner... "said he didn't have to explain himself to any goddam wet-eared deputy. I could see there was trouble brewing, so I reached under the bar for a sawed-off shotgun I keep there, but before I could put my hands on it, the two strangers had managed to get Al Gregg between them, and then this feller drew his gun. Al Gregg wasn't fast enough, and took a bullet in his chest. Not that he would have had a chance anyway, being as the other feller was about to shoot him in the back. But before he could, a man I'd never seen before, but who I found out later was named Martin Davis, came into the saloon, saw what was going on, and shot the other one." Holmgren paused to mop sweat off his face with a bandana, and said apologetically, "It sounds sort of mixed up the way I tell it, but things was happening mighty fast."

"You're doing fine," the judge assured him. "One question: had the deputy, Al Gregg, given any indication of drawing his gun before the accused did?"

"No," Holmgren declared. "Gregg looked surprised as. . . he looked plenty surprised."

"That's a goddam lie!" the prisoner shouted, bounding to his feet. "The deputy went for his gun first. All I did was try to protect myself."

"That's enough," the judge said sharply. "You'll have an opportunity to state your case at the proper time. Until then, you will remain silent."

The sheriff took hold of the prisoner's arm and pulled him down onto the bench. He leaned close to speak to him.

"You heard what the judge said. You won't be doing yourself a favor if you make him mad."

The prisoner muttered something unintelligible, but made no further attempt to get up. Judge Jensen banged his gavel to silence the spectators, who had been aroused by the interruption, then turned to look at the witness.

"You may continue, Mr. Holmgren."

"That's about all," Holmgren said. "The sheriff showed up, somebody went for Doc Yarborough, and by then I was too busy to pay much attention. Seemed like everyone was thirsty."

"Very well," the judge said. He looked inquiringly at the prisoner.

"Do you wish to cross examine the witness?"

"What's the use? He'd just tell a bunch more lies."

With that, Judge Jensen instructed Holmgren to step down, then referred to a list, and called several more witnesses, including the sheriff, Doc Yarborough, and two of the patrons who had been at the saloon. They all corroborated Holmgren's testimony. The judge nodded at the prisoner.

"You may now take the stand, Mr. Doe. The court will listen to your version of the affair."

The prisoner stood up, grudgingly allowed himself to be sworn in, and took the witness chair. It struck the sheriff that he didn't look half as worried as the situation warranted. He seemed as arrogant as ever, and when asked to state his name and occupation, said impudently, "The name's John Doe, and I'm in the banking business."

A titter ran through the crowd, and the prisoner looked smug. Too smug, in the sheriff's opinion. He glanced around at the doorway, and was relieved to see Matt standing there, looking alert. If anything untoward were happening out front, Matt would give him a pre-arranged signal. Somewhat reassured, but still uneasy, the sheriff returned his attention to the prisoner, who was saying boldly, "It's all a pack of lies, just like I figured it'd be. Your stinkin' witnesses had it all lined out what they was going to say. What really happened is that the deputy drew first, and I had to protect myself. That's the honest-to-God truth, so help me."

"Is there anything else you wish to say?" the judge asked. "Because if there is, this is the time to speak up."

"That's all. The word of an honest man against a bunch of conniving liars."

"I see," the judge said. He was silent a moment,

then said solemnly, "Having heard the evidence, it is the verdict of this court that you are guilty of murder, and you are hereby sentenced to be hanged by the neck until dead. Sheriff, you will. . ."

"Oh no, you don't!" the prisoner roared. He leaped out of the chair, and his hand darted inside his shirt, to come out holding a gun. "I'm walking out of here under my own power, and if anyone tries to stop me, it'll be the last thing he does. And in case you think I'm bluffing. . ." He aimed the pistol at Matt, and thumbed back the hammer. "You asked for this, ~~you interfering bastard!~~"

Matt, as surprised as anyone, started to reach for his pistol, then let his hand fall to his side. Even if he could get off a shot in time, which was next to impossible, there would be too much chance of his bullet hitting the judge, who was in the line of fire. He braced himself for the shot he was sure would come.

Everyone in the courtroom seemed turned to stone. Everyone, that was, except the sheriff, who launched himself at the prisoner.

The gun went off, but the sheriff's move had been so unexpected that the prisoner couldn't take time to aim accurately. The bullet went high, tearing a hole in the ceiling. By then the sheriff had wrenched the gun out of the prisoner's hand, and jabbed the muzzle into his stomach.

Pandemonium broke loose, and things didn't return to normal until after the hanging, when Doc Yarborough pronounced the murderer dead. After that the town cleared out rapidly, everyone eager to spread the news. It left the street unusually quiet for a Saturday.

Matt and the sheriff were eating supper at the cafe, waited on by Ellen, who still looked shaken. Matt glanced at the sheriff.

"I haven't really thanked you for saving my life. You could have gotten yourself killed. Why did you do it?"

"Just part of my job," the sheriff shrugged. He wasn't sure himself whether he would have taken the chance had it been anyone other than Matt who was in danger. He frowned thoughtfully, and changed the subject.

"Do you know what's bothering me? Two things, actually. In the first place, how did the prisoner get that gun? Not how, so much, since it must have been passed to him through the cell window, but by whom?"

"Beats me," Matt admitted. "You said there were two things bothering you. What's the other?"

"Well, almost everybody was in town today. Everybody except Ben Gibson and the other small ranchers. They must have had a powerful reason for staying away. I sure wish I knew what it was."

Chapter Sixteen

As Gibson had predicted, there were more people abroad Saturday than on other nights. In fact even more than he had anticipated, since he had not counted on a trial to take them to town.

Although it hadn't been easy, he and Lew Jennings had elicited promises from the other four ranchers to attend a meeting at Double X. It was now nine thirty, and everyone except Dutch Schloemp had shown up. The other five were getting restless, and Hank Debrow put their feeling into words by asking Gibson, "Didn't you say Dutch agreed to come?"

"That's right," Gibson said. "Dutch isn't an easy man to convince, but he finally admitted that we had no choice. He'll be here, all right. However, I reckon we'd better get started without him."

There was a general murmur of approval, and all eyes turned to Gibson, whom they had tacitly accepted as their leader, partly because the meeting was being held in his barn, but mostly because it had been his idea. He cleared his throat and began.

"All of us know what we're up against. We've seen several of our friends crowded out, and at least two of them, for my money, have been murdered. Does anybody doubt that Nolan was in back of it?"

There was no response, and Gibson continued.

"Now there's only the six of us left, and Nolan won't be satisfied until we're gone, too. You know that he tried to get me in trouble with the law by planting some calf hides on my property and telling the sheriff I'd been stealing his beef. His scheme didn't work, but it came too close for comfort. If my girl Laura hadn't spotted that feller near our property, I'd be in ~~one hell of~~ a fix. Maybe even in jail."

They were all watching him intently, and he went on.

"If you're thinking it's just me he's after, you're dead wrong. Probably Lew Jennings has told you what happened to his water tank. There's no way of proving that Nolan's responsible, but we all know that a dirt-walled tank will last for years if it's properly cared for, and I don't reckon anyone's going to accuse Lew of being careless. Have any of the rest of you had trouble? Nels, how about you?"

Nordquest, the oldest man in the group, shook his head.

"Nothing out of the ordinary. To tell the truth, I don't figure my place is big enough for Nolan to bother with."

"That's just what he *wants* you to think," Gibson pointed out. He would have liked to spare Nordquest, on account of his age, but he realized that this would be cruel kindness. "Chances are Nolan might let you alone for a while, so as to lull you into the idea you were safe, but your turn would come, and when it did, you'd have no one left to help you. There's few enough of us as it is; that's why we have to band together. You see that, don't you?"

"I guess so," Nordquest said, with obvious reluctance. Gibson turned to the next man.

"How about you, Will?"

Will Otis, the man he had addressed, said quickly, "Nothing's happened yet, but what you told Nordquest is true. There's just one thing; before I stick my neck out, I'd like to know what you've got in mind. If you're thinking of starting a war against Slash N, you can count me out. We wouldn't stand a chance."

"I'm glad you brought that up," Gibson said. "No, I haven't got any hairbrained idea of charging in like the U.S. Cavalry. According to my reckoning, there's only fifteen of us, counting sons old enough to fight, and hired hands. Also including my girl, who insists on pitching in. Not enough to tackle Nolan's bunch. But we can at least give him something to worry about."

"I ain't sure I follow you," Hank Debrow said.

"All right, I'll give you a for instance. Supposing Nolan pulls a stunt on you like he did on Lew Jennings. The next night, one of Nolan's sheds, or maybe a haystack, goes up in smoke. There's nothing to tie it to you. In fact we'll arrange it so you have witnesses to prove you never left your place."

"Now wait a minute!" Debrow protested. "Nolan ain't going to be fooled that easy. Like as not he'd send some of his crew to burn me out, or do something worse."

"That's a risk we've got to take," Gibson said. "But remember, it could be any one of us as easy as you. Most likely it'd be me, because he's sore on account of that stolen calf deal going sour. So let's put it another way; suppose he blames *me* for the fire and hits *my* place. I'd report it to the sheriff, and we'd have the law on our side."

"Aren't you forgetting something, Ben?" Lew Jennings asked mildly. "Nolan could go to the sheriff, too. I mean if we burned one of his sheds."

"He could," Ben admitted. "But I doubt that he would. He and the sheriff don't see eye to eye, especially after the way that new deputy called his bluff." He stopped talking, and held up a hand for silence.

"Someone's coming. It's likely Dutch Schloemp."

Instead of Schloemp, however, it was Laura who entered the barn. She was a little breathless, as though from running.

"There's something burning over to the west. Come out front and see what you make of it."

For a second no one moved. Then there was a rush for the doorway. All five men stared to the west, where a pink glow lit up the sky.

"It must be the Schloemp place," Gibson said, and ran back into the barn to saddle a horse. The other ranchers' mounts were already saddled, and the men made a run for them. Gibson rode out of the barn, paused only long enough to say to Laura, "You stay close to the house, and be careful. I don't reckon Nolan would hit two places in one night, but you never can tell. This might be just a trick to make me leave the ranch. Keep a gun handy, and if anyone comes close and won't identify himself, don't hesitate to shoot. The way sounds carry at night, I'll hear the shot and come right back."

"Sure, Pa," Laura said. "Don't worry about me. Just take care of yourself." She watched her father ride away at a gallop, then went into the house.

Even before they were close to Schloemp's place, the five riders could smell smoke. Not just the kind made by burning wood, but the sickening odor of burned flesh. Ben Gibson, who had caught up with the others, offered a silent prayer that it would be horseflesh rather than human. His own animal was nervous, so at the edge of the ranchyard he dismounted, tied the reins to a corral post, and ran ahead on foot.

It was the barn, rather than the house, which was ablaze. This gave Ben reason for hope until he realized that Schloemp, if he were alive and able to function, would be fighting the fire. Yet neither he nor his wife Helga nor either of their two sons were in sight.

There was absolutely no chance of entering the barn. The roof had caved in, taking the loft with it, and dumping hay onto the ground floor, where it was burning fiercely. The five men stood transfixed, staring at what was left of the barn, their faces looking unnatural in the flickering light. None of them was able to put his feelings into words, not even Hank Debrow, who was inclined to be voluble.

Ben Gibson was the first to move. Dreading

what he might find, he left the others and approached the house. Habit made him knock, although in this case it was pointless. The door opened to his touch, and he went in.

The kitchen was well illuminated with light from the burning barn. Nothing seemed to have been disturbed. Gibson crossed to an open doorway which led to the parlor. He took one step into the room, and came to an abrupt stop as he saw what he took to be Helga Schloemp's lifeless body sprawled on the floor. He forced himself to move over and kneel down beside it.

Outside, the men heard him yell, and ran to the house. Gibson, still kneeling, said without turning his head. "She's alive, thank God! Go look for the others!" His knife flashed as he cut ropes which were binding the unconscious woman's wrists and ankles. He shook her gently by the shoulders and called her name. After a bit she opened her eyes and stared at him in terror.

"It's all right, Helga. It's me, Ben Gibson."

For a moment the look of terror faded. Then her eyes widened, and she cried something in German, and tried to sit up. The one word Gibson recognized was "Fritz." It took him a second to remember that this was Dutch's Christian name. Helga was the only one who called him that.

Just then Lew Jennings came in from one of the two bedrooms.

"We found the boys. They're all right."

Gibson looked up at him, and Jennings answered the unasked question with a slight shake of his head.

Neither of them had meant for Mrs. Schloemp to

see it, but she once again cried out, "Fritz!" followed by, "Mein Gott!" She started to get up, suddenly went slack, and again lost consciousness.

Gibson stood up and looked at Jennings.

"No sign of Dutch?"

"No," Jennings said. "And I'm afraid there won't be. The boys haven't been able to tell us anything yet, but the bedroom looks like a cyclone hit it, and there's blood on the floor. Are you thinking what I'm thinking?"

Gibson looked down at Helga Schloemp, saw that she was still unconscious, and met Jennings' gaze.

"You mean that what's left of Dutch is in the barn? It looks like it. If he put up a fight, and they, whoever they were, killed him, it would have been a quick way to get rid of his body. God, I wasn't counting on anything like this! Help me lift Helga onto the couch, will you? And ask Otis to ride back to my place and get a wagon. We can't let these folks spend the night here."

Half an hour later they began to get the story of what had happened. Most of it came from the boys, Peter, who was eleven, and Gus, thirteen. Their mother had regained consciousness and was in control of her emotions, but she spoke very little English.

What had taken place, as Ben and the others pieced it together, was that soon after Dutch had left for the meeting, two masked men with drawn pistols had entered the house through the unlocked kitchen door, forced the boys and their mother to submit to being bound, and then set fire to the barn. Apparently, although this was only a guess,

Dutch had seen the smoke and hurried back. He had managed to shoot one of the men in the arm before taking a fatal bullet himself. All this had taken place in the bedroom, under the horrified eyes of the boys, who had been powerless to help. Nor had they recognized the attackers.

The wagon arrived, driven by Laura, who had over-ruled her father's admonition to stay close to the house. She met his eyes without flinching, and said calmly, "Helga Schloemp needs me worse than our house does."

"That's right," her father agreed. "I'm glad you came. The sooner you can get all three of them away from here the better. I'll be along later."

To everyone's relief, Helga didn't refuse to leave the house. She went out with Laura's arm around her shoulders, and the two boys piled into the back of the wagon. By then the fire had died down to glowing embers, though the smell was stronger than ever. Ben turned to the others and said somberly, "You men had better light out for your own ranches. I'll hang around here to make sure a spark doesn't set fire to the house." He glanced at the barn, shook his head, and added, "I was about to say we'd see each other at Dutch's funeral, but if he's in that barn, there won't be anything to bury. I'll get in touch with you later."

They started to turn away, but Ben reached out to touch Lew Jennings' sleeve, and Jennings took the hint and stayed behind. When the others had gone, Ben said grimly, "I guess you're as sure as I am that Nolan was in back of this. Likely he didn't plan on killing Dutch, but he's still to blame. That isn't what I wanted to talk to you about, though.

Can you guess?"

"Yes," Jennings said. "You're wondering how Nolan knew that Dutch wouldn't be at home tonight."

"That's it exactly. Only six of us knew about the meeting. It looks like we might have a traitor in our midst. Any idea which one it could be?"

"No," Jennings said. "Except that I'm dead certain it isn't me." He hesitated, then added, "And equally certain it isn't you."

"That's a relief," Gibson said, smiling for the first time. "With Dutch gone, it narrows down to three, Debrow and Otis and Nordquest. Of course one of them might have let it slip accidentally, but I doubt it. Whoever it was, we've sure as hell got to find out."

Lew nodded, and went for his horse, leaving Ben alone with his somber thoughts.

Chapter Seventeen

Matt and the sheriff had started taking turns at making the final check of the business section, and on the Saturday night of the hanging, the duty was Matt's. It had been an unusually quiet evening, since so many folks who had come to town early for the trial had hurried home to take care of their never-ending chores. Now, at about ten o'clock, the street was deserted, and only the saloon was open. Matt went in, and found the bartender, Bert Holmgren, taking off his apron preparatory to closing.

"Figured I might as well go home," Holmgren volunteered. "I haven't had a customer in an hour. Not that I'm complaining, mind you. I've been busier than a bird dog all day. The trial, and then the hanging, really gave folks a thirst. How about you? Would you like a nightcap?"

"It'd go good," Matt said. "To tell the truth, I'm a little shook up."

"You'd be worse than that," the bartender said. "If it hadn't been for the sheriff."

"I know," Matt agreed, picking up the glass which Holmgren had filled. "It was the damndest thing I've ever seen. I still don't understand why he did it. After all, he's known me only a few days."

"Sometimes a few days can be a long time," Holmgren said.

Matt gave him a questioning look.

"Meaning?"

"Oh, nothing, I suppose. It's just that I've noticed how the sheriff looks at you when you aren't watching, as if you were somebody special. He's a brave man, all right, don't make any mistake about that, but I can't help wondering whether if it had been Al Gregg about to get shot instead of you, the sheriff would have risked his life like he did. After all, when you put on a deputy's badge, you're supposed to take the chances that go along with it."

Matt didn't comment, and Holmgren hurried to add, "Now don't take that wrong. You did all right yourself, just standing there and waiting for it, instead of blazing away and maybe killing the judge. That *is* what kept you from drawing, isn't it?"

"I'm not sure," Matt said. "Maybe I just knew I wouldn't be fast enough."

"Maybe," the bartender said. "But remember, I saw you draw once, that first time you came into the saloon. I reckon you would've had a chance. How about a refill?"

"No, thanks," Matt said. "I'm obliged to you, though. The whiskey may help me go to sleep. Good night."

Out on the street, Matt continued up the block, checking doors, but at the same time pondering the bartender's words, which had brought into focus a question that had been in his own mind. He had never been the type to form a deep attachment for anyone. In fact he had deliberately steered clear of close friendships. Yet after less than a week in Holbrook, there were two chinks in his armor. The first was the sheriff, for whom he had developed a genuine admiration; the second, Laura Gibson, whom he had met on only two occasions, neither of which had been under favorable circumstances. If he didn't watch out, he would be tempted to stay right here in Holbrook.

No, he told himself, that would never do. He had sworn to find his father and avenge his mother. Nothing could be allowed to interfere with that. In the morning, he would turn in his badge and move on.

As he reached this decision, he came to the cafe, and through the window saw Ellen Troup mopping the floor. She spotted him at the same time, and came over to unlock and open the door.

"Come in, Martin. You look as though you could use a cup of coffee."

"Thanks," Matt said, entering the cafe, careful not to step on the freshly mopped part of the floor. "How come you're working so late?"

"You know what they say about woman's work," Ellen said, laughing. "Actually, though, it's mainly because I knew that if I went to bed I couldn't sleep. There's been too much excitement today. I'm certainly glad it's over."

"Me, too," Matt said, sitting at the counter and accepting a cup of coffee. "I didn't see you at the trial."

"No," Ellen said, pouring a cup for herself. "I guess I'm a coward at heart. From what Ed. . . from what the sheriff had told me, I was afraid there might be an attempt to turn the prisoner loose, and if so, I didn't want to see it." She looked at Matt over the rim of her cup. "As it turned out, I wasn't too far wrong, was I? Do you have any idea where the prisoner got that gun?"

"No, except that someone must have passed it to him through the cell window. But I can tell you this much; if it hadn't been for the sheriff, I wouldn't be here drinking your coffee."

"I know," Ellen said. "I bet I've heard the story a dozen times from my customers. It scares me even to think about it."

They were both silent for a few minutes, then Matt ventured to ask, "Have you known the sheriff a long time?"

"Over ten years. That's how long he's been in Holbrook. Why?"

Matt wished he could retract the question. It had sounded too much as though he were prying. He was so slow in answering that Ellen apparently sensed his mood, for she asked gently, "Is something bothering you? If you want to talk about it, I'm a pretty good listener."

"I'm going to quit my job," Matt said bluntly.

He had expected a quick protest from Ellen, but she simply continued to look at him, her expression unchanged. Feeling the need to justify himself, he said lamely, "That was our arrangement, the sheriff's and mine, when I took over as deputy. I told him it wouldn't be permanent. He agreed I could quit any time I wanted to."

"You don't have to explain yourself to me," Ellen said mildly. "The sheriff hasn't tried to talk you out of it, has he?"

"He doesn't know yet. I decided it just a few minutes ago."

"Oh? Did something happen? No, don't answer that. I just got done telling you you didn't have to explain yourself. I'm sure the sheriff won't try to stop you. He's going to feel bad about it, of course. I know that from the way he talks about you. But he won't stand in your way. Does that make you feel any better?"

"No, ~~dammit,~~" Matt said glumly. "I'd feel better if he'd lose his temper and cuss me out. He can't help hating me for quitting, especially when he's just saved my life."

"He won't hate you," Ellen said with conviction. "And as for saving your life, he doesn't look at it that way. He claims he was just keeping his prisoner from escaping."

Matt looked at her for a long moment before saying, "You know something? I don't blame the sheriff for being in love with you. I've never met anyone quite like you before."

Ellen looked both pleased and flustered. She said quickly, "Good heavens, how did we get onto *that* subject? We were supposed to be talking about you."

"I'm sorry," Matt said. "I had no business. . . I mean. . ."

"I know what you mean," Ellen said, smiling as she regained her composure. "But you haven't offended me, if that's what you're thinking. If he loves me, as you seem to believe, I'm not ashamed of it. I just wish. . ."

"Yes?"

"Oh, nothing. Nothing that would interest you, anyway, since you'll be leaving so soon. I wish you luck, wherever you go. And don't worry about Ed. He'll make out somehow. He always does."

Matt nodded, and stood up.

"Thanks for inviting me in. And for the coffee, too. Good night."

"Good night, Martin. Or goodbye, if I don't see you again before you leave."

Back on the street, Matt waited until he heard the bolt being shot home, then crossed to the hotel. His talk with Ellen, instead of relieving his mind, had made him feel worse than before. What sort of person was he, anyway, to walk out on the man whom he had come to respect so highly, and who had saved his life? Had he been making a mistake all these years, putting vengeance above everything else? Damn it, why had he ever come to Holbrook? Until then, he had had no doubts.

A night's sleep on his lumpy mattress did nothing to lift his spirits, and he was up early. He didn't want to face Ellen again, but he still had to confront the sheriff, so he went to the office and let himself in.

Through the window, he presently saw the sheriff walk down the other side of the street and enter the cafe. Somehow, he didn't think that Ellen would report their conversation of the night before. She would give him the opportunity of telling the sheriff himself.

Apparently he was right, for when the sheriff came out of the cafe, his expression was untroubled. He entered the office, smiled at Matt, and said curiously, "Ellen tells me you haven't been in for breakfast yet. Are you feeling all right?"

"I'm fine," Matt said. "I just wasn't very hungry this morning. Besides, there's something I want to talk to you about."

"Oh?" The sheriff went behind his desk and sat down. "I've got something to say, too. Something I think you'll be interested in. Mind if I go first?"

"No, sir," Matt said, secretly relieved at being granted even a brief reprieve. "Mine can wait."

Instead of answering, the sheriff opened a desk drawer, took out one of the WANTED notices, and tossed it face up on the desk. Matt caught his breath as he saw that it was his own. He looked up and saw the sheriff watching him intently.

For what seemed a long time there was no sound except the ticking of the clock. Then Matt said woodenly, "So you finally figured it out."

"I've known since the night you got here," the sheriff said. "You did a pretty good job of changing your appearance, but over the years I've learned to figure out what's behind a man's beard. And of course you made one small mistake; you should have switched to another horse. The one you're riding fits the description on the notice."

"I don't get it," Matt said. "You knew all the time, and yet you didn't lock me up. You even gave me a job. Why?"

"Why? Well, for one thing, the very fact that you hadn't swapped horses indicated to me that you weren't an experienced outlaw, the kind they described in the notice. Also I like to think I'm a fairly good judge of character." He frowned, and added thoughtfully, "Of course there's that part about you wanting to kill your father, but just *wanting* to kill somebody isn't against the law, or I'd have half the town in jail from time to time."

Matt was too dumbfounded to speak, but the sheriff saved the situation by saying mildly, "I suppose you're wondering why I picked this time to let you in on the secret. The explanation is simple enough. I just now found out that you didn't commit the robbery in Gunnison, or murder anyone. The man who did was gunned down while robbing a bank in Denver. He made a deathbed confession, including the part about Gunnison. I read about it a few minutes ago in a Denver paper some drummer left at the cafe."

Matt's relief was so great that he felt almost dizzy. The sheriff looked at him with concern, and asked, "Are you sure you're all right?" He jerked open a desk drawer, took out a bottle, and handed it over. "Take a swig of this."

Some of the liquor ran down Matt's chin, due to his shaking hands, but enough went down his throat to restore him almost to normal. He handed back the bottle, and said embarrassedly, "I'm sorry. I don't usually act like a fluttery old maid."

"Think nothing of it," the sheriff shrugged. "I guess it would have been quite a shock to anybody." He rubbed his jaw reflectively. "You said you had something to talk about, and I haven't given you a chance. What was it?"

"Nothing important," Matt said, uncertain now what he should do, in view of the changed circumstances. He was spared from making a decision by footsteps on the wooden sidewalk, and the sound of the door opening. He turned to see a young boy poised on the threshold, as though undecided whether or not to enter.

Matt had never seen him before, but the sheriff had, and called him by name.

"Come in, Peter. This is my deptuy, Martin. . . no, Matt Dixon. What can we do for you?"

"Ma sent me," the boy called Peter said. "Pa. . . " He was obviously trying to remain calm, but suddenly his resolve melted, and he blurted out, "Pa's dead. They burnt our barn, and. . . "

His voice broke, and tears rolled down his cheeks. The sheriff was out of his chair in an instant, and went over to put an arm around the boy's shoulders.

"Take your time, son."

"Yes, sir," Peter Schloemp said, wiping away his tears with the back of his hand. "It was last night. Pa was gone, and two men busted into the house. They tied up Ma and Gus and me, and set fire to the barn. Pa must've seen the flames, because he came back. They killed him. Afterwards they must've thrown him. . . thrown him. . ."

"That's enough," the sheriff said firmly. "You keep saying 'they.' Did you recognize either of them?"

"No, sir. They were wearing handkerchiefs over their faces. Pa shot one of them, but I don't think he was hurt bad."

"Where's your mother now?"

"At the Gibson's. After the others got there, Laura Gibson came for us in the wagon."

"The others?"

"Yes, sir. There was Mr. Jennings, Hank Debrow, Mr. Otis, Mr. Nordquest, and Mr. Gibson. They all got there while the fire was still burning."

The sheriff looked at Matt.

"I guess now we know why none of them came to the trial."

"Yes, sir," Matt said. "Shall I get our horses?"

The sheriff nodded, and Matt left the office. His decision had been made for him. He couldn't leave the sheriff to handle this new trouble single-handed.

Chapter Eighteen

Matt rode around the corner of the building, leading the sheriff's horse. As he handed over the reins, he asked, "What's become of the boy?"

"He was in a hurry to get back to Gibson's," the sheriff said, stepping into the saddle. "So I told him to go on ahead. It's better that way, anyhow, since I aim to go by the Schloemp place first, and I wouldn't want to put him through that ordeal."

Matt nodded his understanding, and they put their horses in motion. An hour or so later they reached the Schloemp ranch yard. There was nothing left of the barn except cold ashes and charred wood, but an unpleasant odor still pervaded the atmosphere. Both men dismounted and tied their horses, after which the sheriff entered the house, while Matt began poking around in the debris. He was still at it when the sheriff reappeared, and inquired, "Did you find anything?"

"I found this," Matt said, holding out a blackened metal belt buckle.

"It's Dutch's," the sheriff said, after examining it. "He won it years ago in a local rodeo, and wore it all the time. Anything else?"

"Just what you'd expect, some metal parts of harnesses, tools with their handles burned off, and the carcasses of two horses. I also found human bones, which I suppose would have to be Mr. Schloemp's. How about you? Did you turn up anything in the house?"

"Nothing that'll do any good," the sheriff said. "There are a lot of blood stains in one of the bedrooms, and everything is in pretty much of a mess. Of course those five ranchers were here last night, so if there ever was any evidence, which I doubt, I wouldn't be able to recognize it now." He frowned. "One thing keeps bothering me. What became of Dutch's horse, the one he was riding? It wouldn't have been in the barn, so you'd think it would be hanging around."

"Unless the killers took it with them," Matt suggested.

"I sure hope they did. It would give us something to work on. That, and what Peter said about his pa having shot one of the men. Well, there's nothing more we can do here. Let's go to Gibson's and get it over with. I hate like all get-out to face Mrs. Schloemp, but it has to be done sooner or later."

Dutch's widow, however, surprised them by having her emotions under control. She greeted the sheriff politely in her broken English, and acknowledged his introduction of Matt. Evidently she hadn't been so calm at first, for Laura was watching her closely, and paid slight heed to the two lawmen, which Matt found disappointing. She turned her attention to the sheriff, however, when he asked, "Will you be able to put them up for a day or two, until we cover up signs of the fire?"

"Of course, Sheriff. They're welcome to stay as long as they like. I'm afraid it won't be that simple, though. Helga is determined to return to their ranch."

Apparently Mrs. Schloemp had understood

enough to guess what they were talking about, for she said stoically, "We go home now."

When the sheriff would have protested, Laura shook her head.

"It's no use, Sheriff. I've tried every argument I could think of, but her mind's made up. Pa's already hitching a team to one of our wagons. He's going to lend them the rig and horses for as long as they're needed. I offered to go over and stay with them for a while, but Helga turned me down. Politely, of course."

"Well, it's up to her," the sheriff said. "She's probably right, at that. Putting it off would make it that much harder. I'd hoped we could at least clean up what's left of the barn, but maybe it's just as well for them to have something to do to keep busy."

The two boys, Peter and Gus, had been listening quietly, and, at a word from their mother, followed her out of the house. The sheriff took advantage of this opportunity to ask Laura, "Has she said anything about moving away?"

"She says she's staying."

"I guessed as much. I don't suppose she recognized the two men who killed Dutch?"

"No," Laura said. "But she takes it for granted that they were from Slash N. and of course Pa and I do, too. It's the only logical explanation."

From her expression it was evident that she expected some opinion from the sheriff, but he wasn't going to commit himself without solid evidence, so her merely said, "They'll need a new barn before fall. I reckon all the ranchers will pitch in and help."

"All except Nolan," Laura said bitterly.

"Right," the sheriff agreed. "Incidentally, we're going over to his place when we leave here, Matt and me."

"Matt?"

"I forgot," the sheriff said. "You haven't been brought up to date." He smiled, and gestured in Matt's direction. "I'd like you to meet Matt Dixon. You can forget the name Martin Davis. Maybe Matt will explain it to you later, when we have more time."

Laura looked at Matt inquiringly, and he would gladly have taken over the conversation, but the sheriff was already headed toward the door, so Matt simply said, "See you later," and followed him out. Ben Gibson was over by the barn, holding the lines of the team, but the sheriff only waved, and didn't stop to talk. He swung into his saddle, Matt followed suit, and they rode out of the yard.

After they had gone a mile or so, Matt said, "Nolan isn't going to be too happy at seeing me again."

"Does it bother you?" the sheriff asked. "Because if it does, you don't have to go with me."

"I'm not worried," Matt said quickly. "But it might help if I knew your plans. Do you intend to accuse Nolan of burning the Schloemp's barn?"

"Lord no!" the sheriff exclaimed. "Not without any evidence. He'd tell me to prove it, and I'd look foolish." He glanced across at Matt and added, "I didn't mean to jump on you that way, though. Your question made sense. When I was ten years younger, I might have done just what you suggested. However, my reason for going there now is different. In the first place, I want to let him know that he hasn't got us buffaloed. He and I will both understand that I suspect him of being responsible for what happened to Dutch, although we'll both pretend we don't. However, it may worry him a little."

"You said 'in the first place,' " Matt reminded him. "Is there a second reason?"

The sheriff nodded.

"I'm still thinking about Dutch's horse. If you get a chance, take a look around. Also watch for a man who's been wounded. Not that Nolan would be dumb enough to let us find what we're looking for, but the two men who raised all the hell last night might get jumpy, and make a mistake. Unless Nolan has already sent them packing, which I doubt. He won't want to break up his crew, not with trouble in the offing."

"Then you think he knows about the other ranchers getting together?"

"It stands to reason," the sheriff said. "I've a hunch that Schloemp was on his way to a meeting when they set fire to his barn. That's how come the other five ranchers all reached his place so quick. I'd give a month's pay to know who tipped Nolan off."

"Do you suppose one of the ranchers could have double-crossed the others?" Matt asked.

"It's something to think about, but I don't really believe it. Well, here's Nolan's headquarters. Keep your fingers crossed."

"I've been doing that ever since we started over here," Matt said, and automatically loosened the pistol in his holster. Although he had told the sheriff that he wasn't worried, he couldn't forget how Nolan had looked at him on the occasion of their last encounter.

Seeing the Slash N home ranch for the first time, Matt was impressed. The house itself was twice as big as those on other ranches with which he was familiar, and all the other buildings were on the same scale. Everything appeared to be in top shape. Whatever shortcomings Nolan had, he was evidently a good rancher. Either that, or he knew how to hire the right kind of help.

The sheriff had slowed his horse to a walk on entering the ranch yard, and he said in an aside, "Keep your hands in plain sight, and take it slow and easy. There's liable to be some itchy trigger fingers around here, especially if those were Nolan's men who set the fire last night. We don't want to give anybody an excuse to start shooting. There's a watering trough over by the barn, and our horses are probably thirsty. If you should happen to glance into the barn. . . ."

They had almost reached the house, and the sheriff didn't finish the sentence. He dismounted, and handed his reins to Matt, who rode slowly to the barn. Matt heard the sheriff's boots on the veranda, followed by a knock. There was the sound of a door opening and closing, so he deduced that the sheriff had been let into the house.

As Matt neared the barn, a man came out through the wide doorway. Matt, remembering the sheriff's admonition, was careful to keep his right hand well away from his gun. He was relieved when the stranger, who appeared to be in his late forties, regarded him without malice, and said mildly, "Howdy. You lookin' for someone?"

"No," Matt told him. "but I'd like to water these horses, if you've no objections. One of them belongs to Sheriff Durham, who is up at the house. I'm his deputy, Matt Dixon."

"Nate Isaacs," the man said. "Sure, go ahead. You say the sheriff is here? Is something wrong?"

"Not necessarily," Matt said, stepping down and letting the horses drink. He dropped their reins, and moved over toward the barn. "It's hot here in the sun. I'll stand in the shade if you don't mind."

"Help yourself," Isaacs said, but Matt thought that he cast a wary eye at the house, as though anticipating trouble, an impression which was borne out when he added, "Speakin' for myself, that is. I ain't so sure about the boss. Seems like I heard something about you and him having a little ruckus out on the road. He might not like it so well if he was to see me talking to you."

"Oh, it isn't that bad," Matt said. "We didn't have what I'd call a ruckus. And if we had, there's certainly no law against your talking to me."

"Around here, Nolan is the law," Isaacs said rather sourly.

Matt reached the doorway and stepped inside out of the sun. He leaned against a stanchion, took off his hat to wipe sweat from his brow, and said conversationally, "Somehow I get the feeling that you ain't too crazy about your boss. Why don't you go to work for somebody else?"

"Like who?" Isaacs demanded. "All I know is cattle, and there's no other ranches around here except some little ones that won't. . . ." He seemed to catch himself, and broke off short, leaving Matt to guess what he had been about to say. Matt decided it was time to change the subject, so he glanced around at the interior of the barn, and said truthfully, "I've never been in a barn this big before. How many stalls does it have?"

"Twenty four. And believe me it ain't easy keeping 'em all clean. That's my main job now. I ain't up to a full day in the saddle any more. Too many busted bones from being throwed by mean broncs."

Matt had drifted farther into the barn, pretending to be interested in the condition of the stalls, most of which were empty, but secretly keeping an eye open for a horse marked with Dutch Schloemp's Star brand. He was startled when a voice behind him said harshly, "What the hell do you think you're doing, mister? You've got no business here."

The speaker was a tough looking individual wearing a low slung gun. More to the point, he seemed to be favoring his left arm, which he held close to his side.

"Just admiring the barn," Matt said, in what he hoped was a conciliatory tone. "You don't see many this big." He held out his hand. "I'm Matt Dixon."

"I know who you are," the belligerent stranger said. "Even if I was too blind to recognize a deputy's badge when I see one, which I ain't, I saw the sheriff's horse out front. Now get the hell out of here, before I throw you out!"

"With one arm?" Matt jibed. "Mister, I don't know who you are, but you sure as hell don't have good manners."

"Maybe you'd like to teach me some," the man snarled. His gunhand darted toward his holster, and came up holding a pistol.

Quick as he had been, Matt was quicker. His

175

bullet spun the man around, and the gun flew from his fingers. He crashed into a stanchion which was supporting the loft, and slid down to a sitting position. Blood spurted from a new wound in his right arm, and his left arm had also started to bleed. There was venom in the look he gave Matt.

Outside, a door slammed, succeeded by the sound of running feet. Nolan burst into the barn, closely followed by the sheriff. Nolan's eyes flicked to the wounded man, then came to rest on Matt.

"*You* again! By God what have you done this time?"

"Ask *him*," Matt said, gesturing with his left hand toward the wounded man, but keeping his eyes on Nolan. At the edge of his vision, he could see Nate Isaacs backing unobtrusively toward the doorway.

Nolan switched his eyes to the downed man.

"How about it, Ordway? What happened?"

The man he had addressed as Ordway said savagely, "The dirty bastard drew on me for no reason. All I did was ask him what he was doing here in the barn."

"That's a lie," Matt said. "He drew first."

"Do you expect me to take your word over that of a man who's been working for me over a year?" Nolan asked. "Sheriff, I demand that you arrest this man, deputy or not."

"Not so fast," the sheriff said, and Matt risked taking his eyes off Nolan long enough to see that the sheriff had Nate Isaacs by the arm. "Here's a witness to the affair. Let's hear what he has to say."

"All right, damn it," Nolan snapped, and shifted his eyes to the man the sheriff was holding.

"Tell us what you saw, Isaacs."

Isaacs licked his lips nervously, cleared his throat and said hoarsely, "It's like the deputy says. Ordway went for his gun first. He just wasn't fast enough."

"Why you lying bastard!" Nolan roared. "How much did the deputy pay you to back him up?"

"Take it easy," the sheriff cautioned, hardly raising a voice. "It didn't take you and me more than half a minute to get here after the shot was fired. Not enough time for anyone to make a deal." He looked at the wounded man, Ordway.

"I notice both your arms are bleeding. That couldn't be the result of just one bullet."

Before Ordway could answer, Nolan said sharply, "Not that it's any of your business, but he cut his arm on some barbed wire." He turned to glare at Isaacs. "As for you, you've got ten minutes to pack your gear and get going. I won't have a liar working for me."

Isaacs hesitated a moment, then started for the doorway. The sheriff called after him, "If you're going into town, you might as well ride with us. We've accomplished what we came for."

Later, on the way to Holbrook, Isaacs said grimly, "I reckon you saved my life, Sheriff. If I'd ridden out alone, I wouldn't've made it off the ranch. Nolan can't stand being crossed."

"I know," the sheriff said. "And the next time, you may be alone. It mightn't be a bad idea for you to light out. By the way, I don't suppose you know how Ordway really hurt his arm?"

"No. Nobody tells me anything. But I do know this much; his arm was all right yesterday afternoon."

Matt expected the sheriff to ask Isaacs if he knew anything about the attack on Dutch Schloemp's place, but the sheriff let it drop, and it wasn't until some time later, after they were in the office, and Isaacs had left for parts unknown, that he had a chance to ask about it.

The sheriff smiled.

"I knew you were wondering about it, Matt, but look at it this way; supposing Isaacs does know who the two men were, which is doubtful, since he's probably right in saying that nobody tells him anything, how long would his testimony stand up after Nolan produced a dozen witnesses to swear that nobody left the ranch last night? We'd be no better off than before, and Isaacs would be as good as dead. Why rob him of his last chance?"

"I suppose you're right," Matt acknowledged. "But I'm convinced that the man I just shot is the one Mr. Schloemp wounded last night. I hate like the devil to let him get away with it."

"He won't," the sheriff promised. "He's not much better off than Isaacs. Nolan's going to be furious with him for showing himself while you and I were there. Add that to the fact that he won't be much use to anybody with both arms bunged up, and his chances of staying alive are pretty slim. But Ordway and Isaacs aren't the ones I'm worrying about."

"No? Who is?"

"You," the sheriff said bluntly. "Nolan's going to be after your scalp, too. Maybe I should give you the same advice I gave Isaacs."

"You mean run?" Matt asked, and shook his head. "Don't waste your breath, Sheriff. I'm staying."

Chapter Nineteen

While Mrs. Schloemp and her two boys had been at Double X, there had been no opportunity for Gibson to talk privately with Laura. Over the years he had come to rely more and more on her judgement, and as soon as the Schloemps left for their own ranch, he went into the kitchen, waited for Laura to finish drying a cup and turn to look at him, then asked without preamble, "Supposing you were looking for a traitor among the five men who met here last night, which one would you pick?"

Laura looked at him in surprise.

"That's a strange question, but I suppose you had a good reason for asking it. Of course I can eliminate you right off the bat, but as for the others, well, I'd have to give it some study."

"All right," Gibson said. "Think about it. I'll wait."

Laura turned and resumed washing the dishes, but her thoughts were elsewhere. It had never crossed her mind that any of their friends, the small ranchers, would be other than honorable. However, her father wasn't in the habit of asking foolish questions, so she mentally checked off the other four. Lew Jennings could be ruled out almost immediately. Suspecting him would be nearly as bad as suspecting her father.

This left Nels Nordquest, Hank Debrow, and Will Otis. After a bit she faced her father and said, "If I had to pick someone, it would be Hank Debrow, but don't ask me why. He isn't very friendly, but I've never heard anything bad about him."

"I wasn't asking for proof," her father said. "Just for an opinion, which incidentally is the same as mine. I suppose you're wondering what I'm getting at."

"Let me guess. You think somebody tipped off Nolan about the meeting last night. Right?"

Gibson nodded, and Laura continued.

"You're not the only one who's been wondering how those two men knew that Dutch wouldn't be home. It's obvious that they did, or when they didn't find him in the house with his family, they would have gone looking for him. But does that have to indicate that one of the ranchers is a traitor?"

"What do you mean?"

"Well," Laura said. "Any one of them could have leaked the information without meaning to. For instance Nels Nordquest might have let something slip to his hired hand, Sid Liggett. After all, Liggett's been working for him a long time, and they must talk to each other a good deal. It isn't as though Mr. Nordquest would weigh every word he said. And of course he would have had to give Liggett some explanation for leaving the ranch at night."

"That's true," Gibson acknowledged. "And looking at it from that angle, Will Otis could have said something to his man Quillen, or for that matter, Cole Slater might have overheard Lew Jennings discussing it with Martha. And if we're going to include families, there's Lew's boys Ben and Gus, and Hank Debrow's Link." He hesitated, then added reluctantly, "I hate to think of it, but it could even have been one of Dutch's younguns."

"Which means there isn't necessarily a traitor at all," Laura said. "Just someone who got careless. I hope that's the answer, although I hate to think how Dutch's boys must feel if they're responsible for their father's death."

"Yes," her father said soberly. "Well, we won't find the answer by just talking about it."

"What do you intend to do?"

"Nothing, right now. I'm going to pitch in and do my share of the work around here for a change. I've been leaving too much of it up to you."

"I'm not complaining."

"I know. You never do. But you can't continue to run the place single handed, as you have been for the last couple of days. This evening, though, I'll do a little checking around. Probably start at the Jennings's place. Dammit, the way things are going, I hate to leave you alone."

"Don't let that worry you," Laura shrugged. "I'll be all right. Besides, I don't think Nolan would pull the same stunt two nights in a row. Especially now that the sheriff is suspicious of him."

"Speaking of the sheriff," Gibson said, "What do you think of his new deputy?"

"His deputy?" Laura repeated, as though the idea had never entered her mind. "Oh, you mean the one who called himself Martin Davis, but now uses the name Matt Dixon. I haven't really given him any thought."

"I bet you haven't," her father said, grinning. "Well, I'm going to saddle up and ride out to the water tank. After what happened to Lew Jenning's, I plan to keep a close watch on ours. I'll be back around noon."

Laura waited for him to leave the house, then finished the dishes and straightened up the kitchen. She wondered what had prompted his question about the deputy. Were her inmost thoughts so easy to read? The idea was disconcerting.

She also wondered about the change of names. Why would a man who called himself Martin Davis suddenly become known as Matt Dixon? The use of assumed names wasn't too uncommon in this part of the country, but it generally indicated that the person had something to hide. To herself she admitted that she hoped it wasn't true in this case. But if it *was*, or even if it *wasn't*, for that matter, what had induced him to resume what was supposedly his true identity?

Well, she told herself sternly, it was certainly no concern of hers. He could call himself George Washington for all she cared. There were more important things to think about. She flung the dish towel over the back of a chair, and hurried out of the house, letting the door slam behind her.

As her father had promised, he was back at the house in time for the noon meal. He had found nothing wrong with the water tank, nor with anything else, except that a few head of Slash N cattle had wandered onto Double X land. He had hazed them back across the line, and driven some of his own cows back where they belonged.

The rest of the day passed uneventfully, with both Gibson and Laura too busy to do much talking. This suited Laura, for she didn't want to answer any more questions about Matt Dixon. After supper, with the chores out of the way, her father again saddled up and rode out. By then it was almost dark, and neither of them saw the man who was lying prone behind a small hill, peering at the ranch yard. Soon after Gibson left, the unseen spy backed off, mounted a horse which had been tied out of sight, and rode in the direction of Slash N.

The rider, Dakota Groves, was soon knocking on Nolan's door, which was opened by Nolan, who had been expecting him. Nolan looked inquiringly at Groves, and the latter nodded.

"Gibson just left the ranch. Shall I. . . "

Nolan didn't give him time to finish the sentence, but said curtly, "You already know what you're supposed to do. Get moving!"

Groves' countenance was impassive, but he was mentally cursing Nolan as he left the house, mounted his horse, and took off. Immediately afterward, Nolan put on his hat, also left the house, and crossed to the bunkhouse. Several members of his crew were already in their bunks, but four were playing poker, and the foreman, Dyke Blodgett, was doing some figuring in a tally book. Nobody spoke, but the poker players stopped play to look at Nolan curiously, since it wasn't his habit to associate with the help. Dyke Blodgett stood up, pocketed the tally book, and stepped over to the doorway.

"Something you want, Mr. Nolan?"

Without answering, Nolan left the bunkhouse, motioning for Blodgett to follow. When they were outside, Nolan said brusquely, "Saddle my horse, and one for yourself. We're going to take a ride."

Blodgett nodded, and headed for the horse barn. He was vaguely uneasy about this unplanned excursion, especially in view of what had happened at Dutch Schloemp's place the night before. What little he knew about the burning of Schloemp's barn, and the killing of Dutch, had come to him second hand, since he hadn't been in on the deal, but Ordway's explanation of how he had hurt his arm had been a little too glib. It didn't ease his mind when he and Nolan, after mounting, set off in the direction of Ben Gibson's Double X.

Blodgett was a naturally taciturn man, and particularly so with Nolan, so he kept his worries to himself. He had never refused to follow Nolan's orders, and could continue to do so if at all possible, but if Nolan proposed any violence against Gibson or his daughter, he would balk.

Fortunately, it didn't become necessary to make this drastic move, for when they came within hailing distance of the house, Nolan reined up and called loudly, "Gibson? This is Nolan. I want to talk to you."

Inside the house, Laura was already aware that someone was approaching, for her sensitive ears had caught the soft thud of hoofs and the jingle of bit chains. She had doused the light, discarded the shotgun in favor of a rifle, which had a greater range, and gone outside to stand in the dark area next to the house. Her eyes, accustomed to the gloom, made out the shapes of the two riders, and at the sound of Nolan's voice, which no one could fail to recognize, she called back. "Get off your horses and walk in real slow. Pa's got you covered from the barn, so don't try anything cute!"

Nolan muttered something which Laura fortunately didn't catch, but after a brief hesitation, there was the creak of saddle leather as the men dismounted, then they moved up on foot close enough so that Laura was able to recognize the second man as Dyke Blodgett. This was a relief, for she had always considered him one of the few decent members of the Slash N crew. It did not, however, keep her from ordering, "Now lay your guns on the ground."

"Dammit," Nolan grumbled. "Don't you know who I am?"

"Yes," Laura said. "I know you only too well, Mr. Nolan." She tilted the barrel of her rifle. "Including the fact that you have a pistol on you, even though it probably doesn't show. Either lay it down, or climb back on your horse and get off our property."

Nolan apparently had control of himself, for he said resignedly, "All right, there's no reason to get hostile." He reached under his coat and produced a revolver, which he laid carefully on the ground. As he straightened up, he added, "We didn't come here looking for trouble. I just want to talk to your pa."

The Slash N foreman, without saying anything, drew his own gun and bent down to place it beside Nolan's. Laura had the impression that there was a smile on Blodgett's face, but in the dim light she couldn't be sure. He straightened up, and Laura, still holding the rifle steady, moved aside so as not to block the path to the back door.

"We can go inside now. Mr. Blodgett, would you please go first and light the lamp?"

"Yes'm," Blodgett said. He passed Laura and entered the house, and in a moment light spilled from the doorway.

"You next, Mr. Nolan."

Nolan went through the doorway, and Laura followed. She had the uncomfortable feeling that she might be walking into a trap, but both men kept their distance, and didn't sit down until she invited them to. She remained standing, her back to a windowless wall.

"Just why did you really come here, Mr. Nolan?"

"Why, it's like I said," Nolan told her. "I wanted to talk to your pa." He smiled, and added, "Only he isn't here, is he? What you said about him being in the barn was a bluff. I've got to hand it to you, girl; you're a cool customer. You even had me fooled for a minute."

Laura chose not to answer, and after a bit Nolan said, "I suppose there's no use asking where he is?"

"You suppose right," Laura said, and Nolan's smile broadened.

"Then let me put it this way; how soon do you expect him back?"

"I'm quite sure that's none of your business," Laura said, and was surprised that Nolan showed no annoyance. Instead, he seemed very well pleased with himself. His smugness worried her. Was he keeping her occupied so as to give others of his crew time to commit some devilment? She let her glance shift to Blodgett, but there was nothing in his expression to give her a clue. She returned her attention to Nolan.

"This isn't going to get us anywhere. If you want to leave a message for my father, I'll see that he gets it."

Nolan appeared to consider this a few seconds, then shrugged.

"All right. I just wanted to assure him that I had nothing to do with what happened to Dutch Schloemp last night. It has crossed my mind that some of the other ranchers might blame me for it, and do something to get even. I'd like your father to stop them. If there's one thing we don't need around here, it's trouble between us cattlemen."

"I'll tell him what you've said," Laura promised. "And now, I think you'd better leave." She moved to one side so as to leave an open passage to the doorway.

Nolan rose to his feet, nodded, and said mildly, "Whatever you say, Miss. Good night."

Laura didn't answer, but waited for them to leave the house, followed them out, and watched them pick up their weapons, return to their horses, and ride away. The visit had left her confused and angry, and she felt that she hadn't handled herself very well. Even after checking the barn and other buildings and finding nothing wrong, she wasn't satisfied. She didn't believe for a minute that Nolan had ridden this far at night for the reason he had given. Had something happened to her father? The thought made her shudder.

It was well past midnight when he returned, tired and disgusted. In response to her question, he said grimly, "I didn't even *get* to the Jennings place, dammit. About halfway there, I was waylaid."

"You aren't hurt, are you?" Laura asked

anxiously.

"Only my pride. I should have been more careful. The skunk that stopped me stayed in the shadow of a clump of cedars, and all I could see was the barrel of his rifle. He made me get down, took my six shooter, and ordered me to start walking. I heard him ride off leading my horse. By the time I found the horse again, there was no point going to the Jennings's. Besides, I was anxious to make sure you were all right. Are you?"

"I'm fine," Laura said. "But something strange happened here, too. Nolan and his foreman paid us a visit."

"They didn't. . ."

"Oh, they behaved like perfect gentlemen," Laura said. "Of course that might have been partly because I had a gun and they didn't, but I don't think Nolan meant me any harm, and I'm sure that Dyke Blodgett didn't. Nolan left you a message. He said to tell you he had nothing to do with the trouble at Dutch Schloemp's last night, and he wants you to keep the other ranchers from doing anything violent."

"That doesn't sound like Nolan," Gibson said. "I'm the last person he'd come to for a favor. I wish I knew what he was really up to."

"So do I," Laura said. "But I'm sort of afraid to find out." She forced a smile. "You must be tired, and I know I am. Good night."

"Good night," her father said, but he doubted that it would be.

Chapter Twenty

Nolan had eaten breakfast alone at seven o'clock, and now, almost three hours later, he hadn't left the house. In his state of mind it had seemed like six hours rather than three, and he was pacing the floor like a caged animal. When at last there was a knock at the door, he almost groaned with relief. However, he held himself in check for a few seconds before answering the knock.

One of his crew, a man by the name of Riker, was on the doorstep. He started to blurt out something, but Nolan, who had assumed an expression of surprise, interrupted him.

"Not so fast, man. Take a deep breath and start over. Just what is it you're trying to tell me?"

"The cattle, boss, a bunch of them are dead."

"Dead?" Nolan repeated, looking properly perplexed. "Do you mean they got into loco weed or something?"

"They're in that arroyo up by the big Joshua tree. Something must've stampeded 'em during the night."

"Something?" Nolan echoed. "That's crazy! We didn't even have lightning or thunder last night. If they stampeded, it was because somebody wanted them to. Go saddle my horse. . . no, I'll do that myself. You find Dyke Blodgett and tell him to meet me at the arroyo. He's over west a piece."

Riker nodded, and ran toward his horse, which was lathered from having been ridden so hard.

Nolan, once he had reached the privacy of the barn, smiled with satisfaction as he saddled his horse. However, when he rode out, he looked appropriately grim. He was still maintaining this tight-lipped posture when Blodgett joined him at the edge of the arroyo, where he was staring down at the carcasses of about fifty head of Slash N stock, and watching two of his men put several cripples out of their misery. Blodgett's expression was a mirror of his own, and the foreman's voice was hoarse as he asked, "Have you figured out what happened?"

Nolan tore his gaze off the gory scene below, and turned to look at him.

"I've figured what *didn't* happen. They didn't stampede on their own. Somebody spooked 'em, and I've got a damned good idea who it was."

Blodgett looked at him soberly for a long minute without answering, and Nolan said impatiently, "Go ahead and say it. You know who I'm talking about, that bastard Gibson. This is what he was doing last night when we were at his house. No wonder the girl wouldn't tell us where he'd gone."

"He couldn't have done it alone," Blodgett said. "Not this big a bunch."

"So he had help," Nolan said, as though it made no difference. "Likely it was one of the other ranchers, but Gibson's still the ringleader. Do you agree, or don't you?"

Blodgett thought about it a moment. He had never considered Ben Gibson the kind of man who would deliberately drive a herd of cattle to their death, but maybe if he became desperate enough. . .

"It looks like it, Mr. Nolan, but I'd feel better if we had some kind of proof other than the fact that he wasn't home last night."

Nolan made an angry gesture.

"Personally, I've got all the proof I need, but if it'll make you feel any better, let's look around and see what we can find. His horse might have left some prints we can identify; maybe it has an odd-shaped shoe or something. We'd better split up. That way we can cover more ground."

Blodgett nodded, waited for Nolan to start off, then reined his horse in the other direction. The ground was so badly churned by the stampeding cattle that he had slight expectation of finding any identifiable prints, but it at least postponed what he feared would be a showdown with Ben Gibson, and its probably violent consequences. Having worked most of his life with cattle, Blodgett shared Nolan's anger at this wanton destruction. On the other hand. . .

A glint of sunlight caught his eye, and he rode over for a closer look. It proved to be a reflection from the barrel of a revolver, and when he got down and picked it up, what he saw put a bitter taste in his mouth. He called to Nolan, who had been searching in another direction. Nolan took the revolver which Blodgett held up to him, looked at it a moment, and said with certainty, "By God this clinches it! Only Gibson's gun would have the initials 'B.G.' carved in the grips. We don't have to waste any more time here. In fact he may have skipped out already. Round up some of the men and follow me."

Laura and her father were just finishing their noon meal when they heard horses approaching. Laura looked out the window, and said uneasily, "It's Nolan and his foreman, and this time there's a bunch of Slash N men with them." She reached for the shotgun, but her father stopped her.

"Leave it be. We wouldn't have a chance against that many, and all they'd need would be to see us holding guns to start 'em shooting. I'll go out and see what it's all about. They ain't likely to start anything, especially as I'm wearing an empty holster."

Laura recognized the logic of what he was saying, and didn't follow him out, but she picked up a rifle, levered a cartridge into the chamber, and took up a position beside the window. If her father was wrong, if anyone drew a gun, she would blast Nolan out of his saddle.

Nolan, however, had different plans, for he signalled the others to stop, and after riding a short distance ahead of them, reined up his own mount. He waited a few seconds, possibly expecting Laura to appear, then fixed his gaze on Gibson.

"What made you do it, man? You must've known you couldn't get away with it."

"It?" Gibson said. "What're you talking about?"

"Oh, come off it," Nolan snorted. "You know what I mean. However, if you want it spelled out, you stampeded a bunch of my cattle over the edge of an arroyo."

"That's a damned lie!" Gibson exploded. "I don't know what kind of crazy deal you've cooked up, but it won't work. Take your bunch of owlhoots and get off my property!"

Nolan smiled thinly.

"We'll get off, all right, but you're going with us."

"Going where?" Gibson demanded.

"Why to see your good friend the sheriff," Nolan told him. "Only this time even he can't let you off easy. Not with all the evidence against you."

In spite of himself, Gibson was beginning to sweat. Nolan's air of extreme confidence was unnerving.

"What evidence?"

"Well, first off, you were away somewhere last night when it happened, and your girl wouldn't tell us where, me and my foreman. That looks pretty suspicious in itself, especially when you consider that she held a gun on us all the time we were there. Isn't that right, Blodgett?"

"Yes, sir," Blodgett said, without enthusiasm.

"Besides, which," Nolan went on implacably, "I notice you aren't wearing a pistol. Do you want me to tell you why? It's because you lost it last night. Lost it within a hundred yards of the spot where the cattle went over the edge. No, I didn't find it. Dyke Blodgett did."

Gibson looked at Blodgett, who nodded. He let his gaze move over the rest of the bunch, and counted six others. He hoped to God that Laura, who must be listening to this, wouldn't do anything rash. To forestall this, he said loudly enough for her to hear, "All right, Nolan, you've done a good job of framing me. Lots better than you did with the calf-hides. Tell your men to take their hands off their guns. I'll go with you to town, and you can repeat your lies to the sheriff. I reckon he'll figure out what you're up to."

"Now you're using your head," Nolan said. He beckoned to one of his men. "Go saddle him a horse. Gibson, you stay right where you are. And if that girl of yours is looking, she'd better not start anything. Understand?"

Gibson nodded, waited for his horse to be led out, and swung into the saddle. Flanked by Nolan, and followed by the others, he rode off toward Holbrook. He wasn't at all sure he would reach town alive, but at least nothing had happened to Laura. Not yet, anyway.

Matt was holding down the office when the group pulled up out front. He stepped to the doorway, and was met by an icy stare from Nolan, who said arrogantly, "Tell the sheriff I want to see him."

Before responding to this command, Matt looked at Ben Gibson, and was shocked at how much the man had changed since yesterday. He also noted the empty holster, and could guess that Gibson wasn't here of his own free will. Gibson didn't say anything, however, and Matt's eyes came to rest on Nolan.

"The sheriff isn't here. Maybe I can do something for you."

"No chance," Nolan said coldly. "I've already had a sample of how you work. Why isn't the sheriff around when he's needed?"

Matt's lips thinned, but before he could answer, the man under discussion came out of the feed store next door, took in the situation at a glance, and said evenly, "Being sheriff doesn't mean sitting in the office all day. What's your problem?"

"Him," Nolan said, pointing at Gibson. "Only he's not *my* problem any more, he's *yours*. I tried to warn you about him before, but you wouldn't listen. This time he hasn't just stolen a couple of my calves; he's killed about fifty head of my steers."

"Oh?" the sheriff said. He looked at Gibson a minute, then added with deep irony, "I take it he's a pretty dangerous man, since it took you and half your crew to bring him to town. And him without a gun, at that. I think three or four of us should be able to handle him. Suppose you have the rest of your army wait for you in the saloon."

Nolan obviously didn't like this, but he turned to his crew and said flatly, "You men hang around town until I'm ready to go back. Blodgett, you stick with me. You know why."

Blodgett nodded, and swung down from his saddle. The sheriff gestured to Gibson, who also dismounted, as did Nolan. The five of them, Gibson, Blodgett, Nolan, the sheriff, and Matt, filed into the office, where the sheriff settled himself behind his desk.

"All right, Mr. Nolan, let's have your story."

"It isn't a story, damn it," Nolan snapped. "Just the honest-to-God truth. Sometime last night a bunch of my Slash N cattle were stampeded over the edge of that arroyo on my place. Most of them were killed outright. A few were crippled and had to be shot. According to a quick count, I lost around fifty head." He glanced at Blodgett. "Isn't that about what you made it?"

"Close enough," Blodgett agreed.

"All right," the sheriff said. "Let's assume you're right as to the number. How does Mr. Gibson enter into it?"

"God-damn it, he's the cause of it all! Maybe he had a little help, but it was his doing."

The sheriff looked at Gibson, but Gibson didn't say anything, so he turned back to Nolan.

"I suppose you can prove this?"

"I sure as hell can," Nolan said. "Unless you're too prejudiced to listen. In the first place, we all know that Gibson has it in for me, on account of some fool idea that I'm trying to crowd him off the range. Last night I rode over to his place, hoping to patch things up. My foreman, here, was with me. Tell him about it, Blodgett."

Blodgett didn't appear to like being put on the spot, but he said evenly, "It's like Mr. Nolan says, Sheriff, I mean about us going over to Double X last night. Mr. Gibson wasn't home, and his girl, Laura, wouldn't say where he was or when he'd be back."

"Tell him the rest of it," Nolan prompted.

"Yes, sir. The Gibson girl was waiting for us with a rifle, which seemed sort of odd. She made us lay down our guns, and kept us covered all the time we were there. When it became clear that she wasn't going to tell us anything, we went back to the ranch."

Blodgett's eyes had not shifted from the sheriff's as he talked, and his apparent honesty impressed the sheriff much more than Nolan's bluster. Was it possible that Gibson was really guilty? The sheriff turned toward Nolan.

"All right, I'll take your foreman's word that Gibson wasn't home, and that the other things are true. You still haven't tied Gibson to the stampede."

"I was waiting for you to get around to that," Nolan gloated. "Blodgett, tell him what you found near the arroyo."

Blodgett nodded, and said tonelessly, "I found a Colt forty-five. It had the initials. 'B.G.' carved on the grips."

"And here it is," Nolan said triumphantly, producing the gun which was stuck in his waistband, and stepping up to lay it on the desk. "Maybe your friend Gibson would like to lie his way out of *this*."

Matt watched in disbelief as the sheriff picked up the gun and examined it. It seemed impossible that Gibson could be guilty of such a crime, but so far he hadn't said a word in his own defense.

"Is this your gun?" the sheriff asked Gibson, and the latter nodded.

"It's mine, all right. But I didn't lose it near Nolan's arroyo, or anywhere else on Nolan's land. In fact I didn't lose it at all. It was taken away from me."

Nolan started to interrupt, but the sheriff motioned him to silence.

"You've had your chance to talk, and Mr. Gibson didn't butt in. Now I want to hear what he has to say. Ben, let's have it."

"Sure, Sheriff, but I can tell you right now that I don't have anybody to back me up. It's like Nolan says, I wasn't home last night. I started over to Lew Jennings' place, never mind what for, and halfway there, I was ambushed. Well, not ambushed exactly, because nobody shot at me. But I was stopped by a man holding a rifle. He made me dismount, took that pistol away from me, and told me to start walking. He left, riding his own horse and leading mine. He must have led it quite a ways, because I didn't find it for a couple of hours. By then it was too late to go to Jenning's, so I rode home, and got there after midnight. I reckon that's about the size of it."

The ensuing silence was broken by Nolan who asked sarcastically, "This mysterious rider who waylaid you... did you recognize him?"

Gibson ignored the question until the sheriff said reasonably, "That's something you'll have to answer sooner or later, Ben. Did you?"

"Hell no! I didn't even get a good look at him. He kept to the shadow of a clump of cedars."

"Well, Sheriff?" Nolan asked. "Are you going to swallow a cock-and-bull story like that, in face of all the evidence against it? Or are you going to do your duty and lock Gibson in a cell?"

The sheriff looked at Gibson bleakly.

"Lord knows I hate to do this, Ben, but I've got no choice. You can see that, can't you?"

"I reckon," Gibson said. "It looks like this time he's got me framed for sure. I'd appreciate it, though, if you'd check it out yourself."

"I will," the sheriff promised, and turned to

face Nolan.

"You can go now. If I need any more information, I'll let you know."

Nolan gestured to Blodgett, and they left the room. Matt stepped to the doorway and watched them cross the street and go into the saloon. He turned to see Gibson entering the cell. The sheriff closed the iron barred door carefully, locked it, put the key in his pocket, and looked at his prisoner.

"If it's any comfort to you, Ben, I think you were telling the truth. Proving it is going to be something else, but I'll do my best."

"I know you will," Gibson said. "There's one other thing I'd like you to do for me. Laura's out there on the ranch alone, wondering what's happening to me. I'm afraid for her."

"I'll take care of it," the sheriff said. He thought a moment, then turned to Matt.

"Matt, I'd like for you to ride out to Gibson's place. Tell Laura how things stand, and try to persuade her to come to town. I know she'll be welcome to stay at Ellen's."

"And if she refuses?"

"In that case, use your own judgement," the sheriff said.

"Yes, sir," Matt told him. He didn't consider it necessary nor advisable to add that he had already made up his mind to go out to Double X before the sheriff had told him. Nor did he stop to wonder why he should be so concerned about a girl he hardly knew. Without wasting time, he left the office, mounted his horse, and set out on the road to the Gibson ranch.

Chapter Twenty-One

Once again, Laura was holding the shotgun when Matt rode in, but on recognizing him, she leaned the gun against the side of the house and moved away from it. Her expression was troubled, which was not surprising, and her first words were about her father.

Matt hastened to reassure her, insofar as he could.

"Your pa's all right. He was talking with the sheriff when I left."

She seemed momentarily relieved, then frowned and asked suspiciously, "If he's all right, why didn't he come back to the ranch?"

"What I mean," Matt explained, "is that he's in good shape physically." He tried to think of a painless way of telling her the rest, gave up, and said frankly, "He's in jail."

"In jail! Do you mean to tell me the sheriff believed all those lies of Nolan's?"

"No, but considering the evidence. . . hey! Where are you going?"

Laura, who had abruptly picked up the shotgun and started toward the barn, said over her shoulder, "To town, of course, to get my father out of jail. If no one else is willing to help, I'll do it myself."

Matt caught up, grabbed her by the shoulder, and swung her around. An emotion which had been building for some time burst its bounds, and he said roughly, "Don't be stupid! What do you intend to do, tear the jail apart stone by stone? Or maybe you mean to kill the sheriff and take his keys. Damn it, don't you realize he's going to do everything possible to get your pa out of this mess? Can't you trust him a little?"

"I don't trust anybody anymore, not even the sheriff. Or you, either, for that matter! How can I be sure you aren't secretly on Nolan's side? I don't even know who you are. Martin Davis? Matt Dixon? It's pretty hard to trust a man who keeps changing his name."

Matt let go of her shoulder, but something in his expression evidently impressed her, for instead of hurrying toward the barn, she said contritely, "I shouldn't have said that. I'm sorry."

"You needn't be," Matt told her. "In your place, I guess I'd feel the same way. I probably can't convince you that I'm not double-crossing you and your pa, but I can at least explain about the two names. If you're interested, that is, and have time to listen."

Laura didn't turn away, and Matt took this as a favorable sign. He hadn't intended to discuss his personal affairs with anybody, but for some reason Laura's opinion of him was very important. Of course once she learned the truth, that opinion might hit rock bottom. Nevertheless he continued.

"When I came to Holbrook, I was running from

the law. Folks up in Colorado thought I had pulled a robbery in which an innocent man was killed. The Gunnison town marshal locked me in a cell, and made it plenty clear that I'd be found guilty and hanged. To make it short, I managed to get hold of the marshal's gun, left him tied and gagged in the cell, and lit out. I grew a beard to change my appearance, and started using the name Martin Davis. After dodging the law for about a month, I came to Holbrook because my horse went lame, and Holbrook happened to be the nearest town. You know what took place the night I arrived. When the sheriff offered me a job, I thought it would be a good way to hide out until they quit looking for me."

Laura was listening intently, and there was no longer any animosity in her expression. Matt waited a moment for her to comment, then hurried on.

"I didn't find out until later that the sheriff knew who I was the first time he looked at me. Even after I found a WANTED notice for me in his desk, I was dumb enough to think he hadn't recognized me from my description."

Laura frowned in a puzzled way.

"If he knew who you were, why didn't he. . . "

"Arrest me?" Matt said. "Lord knows I've spent a lot of time trying to figure that out, even since he gave me what he considered a reasonable explanation, simply that I didn't look or act like the sort of person who'd do the things they'd accused me of."

"And he still has no intention of turning you in?"

"No, but there's a good reason for it now. You see, the sheriff picked up a Denver paper someone had left in the cafe, and found an item telling about a robbery in Denver. The man who committed it was shot and captured. In a death-bed confession, he admitted being the one who had pulled the Gunnison robbery, and shot the man I was accused of killing."

"How awful!" Laura said. "I mean you being in jail, knowing you were about to be executed for something you hadn't done. Thank goodness the sheriff trusted his instincts. You must be terribly relieved."

"I am," Matt said. "But you may as well hear the rest. For the last few years I've been trying to find my father, who deserted my mother when I was just a baby. I've sworn to kill him."

"Oh no!" Laura gasped. "Kill your own father? I don't believe you could do it. I mean. . . "

"I know what you mean," Matt said soberly. "But I've never thought of him as my father, not the way you do yours; he's just a man who ran out on my mother when she needed him. I don't suppose I can make you understand."

"No," Laura said. "You can't. But it's between you and your conscience. Does the sheriff know this, too?"

Matt nodded.

"He must. Like a fool, I told everybody I met, including a town marshal in Colorado, so of course it was on the WANTED notice. Well, now you know. Thanks for listening. Are you still fixing to ride into town? Because if you are, I won't try to stop you."

"What do you think I should do?" Laura asked, and Matt looked at her in wonder.

"Do you mean that in spite of what I've just told you, you'd still listen to me?"

"Of course," Laura said simply.

"Well, if you really want to know, I think you can do your pa a lot more good right out here. Or *we* can, if you'll let me help. Will you?"

Laura nodded, and Matt continued.

"In the first place, we can try to find the spot where your pa was waylaid. There ought to be the tracks of two horses, your pa's and the other man's. It's worth looking into, don't you think?"

"It's a lot better than doing nothing," Laura agreed. She smiled wryly. "Or riding into town like an avenging angel, which is what I'd be doing right now if you hadn't stopped me." Her smile faded as she turned serious. "Pa was on his way to the Jennings place when it happened. I believe I know the route he would have taken." She hesitated. "Of course he made me promise not to leave the ranch, but I think this is one time I'd be justified in breaking my word. I'll go saddle a horse."

With Laura pointing out the way, they rode out toward Lew Jennings' ranch. After they had gone a mile or so, Matt recalled something he had heard in town, but had not considered important at the time.

"Your pa said the man who stopped him was hiding behind a clump of cedars. Does that mean anything to you?"

"It certainly does," Laura said. "Of course there's more than one spot that fits that description, but not on the trail I think pa would have taken. Let's go." She touched spurs to her horse's flanks, and the animal took off at a gallop, not slowing until they came within sight of her apparent destination. She gestured ahead.

"That's it, if it's the right one."

Matt dismounted, handing her his reins.

"I'll go the rest of the way on foot. If there are any hoof prints, we don't want to muddle them with those of our own horses."

Laura nodded, and Matt walked ahead, scanning the ground. He soon found a clear set of hoofprints headed in the direction he and Laura were going. Near the clump of cedars, the prints became jumbled, as though the horse had milled around. Beyond the cedars there were additional prints, and a discarded cigarette butt. Whoever had lain in wait for Ben Gibson had been either careless or extremely confident. Farther on, the prints of two horses angled off to the west. Matt hurried back to where Laura was waiting.

"This is the spot, all right. There's two sets of hoofprints heading off that way." He pointed. "What's over there?"

"Nothing," Laura said. "Nothing I can put a name to, that is. There aren't any ranches in that direction, and not even any decent grazing land. After a couple of miles, it's mostly bare rock. I'm told even the Indians avoided it. All it's good for is rattlesnakes and scorpions."

"And a rider who doesn't want to leave any trail," Matt said. "From what you say, there'd be no point following the prints. Whoever ambushed your pa could have kept to the bare rock for a while, and then headed any way he wanted to."

"Which would have been to Slash N," Laura said positively. "That's where we ought to go, too."

"You're right," Matt told her. "Only it's not 'we.' I'm going alone.

"Oh no you're not! I'm in this as deep as you are. Deeper, because it's my father who's in jail. If you won't let me go with you, I'll go my myself."

Before answering, Matt stepped into his saddle. Laura's chin was thrust out, and her eyes blazed defiance. He knew that it would be useless to argue with her in this mood, but somehow he had to keep her from riding into danger. Holding his voice low, he said reasonably, "You're absolutely right. He's your pa, and you want to do what's best for him. So do I, but I don't think the two of us can take on Nolan's outfit. He had half a dozen of his men in town with him, and since they were in the saloon, they may still be there, but that leaves at least as many more to reckon with."

Laura's anger subsided, and she asked dubiously, "If two of us aren't enough, how do you propose to do anything by yourself?"

"I don't," Matt told her. "That is, I don't intend to tackle Nolan's crew if they're at the ranch. But I can stay out of sight and scout around. Then when you get there with the others, we'll know what to do."

"The others? I don't understand. What others?"

"Why the ranchers, of course," Matt said matter-of-factly. "That's what you'll be doing, rounding up your friends." He glanced at the sky. "By the time you get them together, it'll be almost dark. The bunch of you can sneak up on Slash N without being spotted."

Laura regarded him speculatively, and he had almost decided that she would reject the idea, when she finally said, "All right. You're probably more experienced at this sort of thing than I am. Please be careful."

"I will," Matt promised, although he had faint hope of avoiding trouble. He wanted to say more, but decided against it.

Laura started to ride away, reined up, and turned to look back over her shoulder.

"I really am sorry for what I said back there. About not trusting you, I mean."

"Forget it," Matt said, and set out quickly in the direction of Slash N. Laura's words had raised his hopes. Maybe...

That could wait. When he saw her again, he could reveal how he felt about her. *If* he saw her again, he reminded himself. Lord knew what would happen when he reached Slash N, especially since he had no intention of just scouting around as he had indicated to Laura. Nor did he anticipate that Lew Jennings and the other ranchers would come to his assistance. Sending Laura to enlist their help had been a ruse to keep her out of danger. This was a one-man job, and it was up to him to do it.

Chapter Twenty-Two

Although he had visited the Slash N headquarters only once, Matt had a countryman's sense of direction which enabled him to find it again without difficulty. A thread of smoke rising against the blue sky told him when he was close, and he dismounted, tied his horse to a shrub, and went ahead on foot, keeping out of sight of the house by staying behind a ring of low hummocks which encircled the ranch yard.

He crawled the last few yards on his stomach, and cautiously raised his head to peer over the rise. He had intentionally chosen a spot where the westering sun would be at his back, and was hopeful that anyone chancing to look his direction would be blinded by the glare.

Oddly enough, there was no one in sight. Had it not been for that smoke rising from the chimney, he might have thought the place deserted. Instantly suspicious, Matt flung a quick look over his shoulder, afraid that he might have been lured into a trap. However, there was no sign of life except for his horse, which was standing hip-shot where he had left it. Still not completely satisfied, he backed away from the ridge, made a quarter-circle around the yard, and inched up for another look, this time in such a position that the big barn was between himself and the other buildings.

Had Matt known it, there was a simple explanation for the lack of activity around Slash N. The men who had accompanied Nolan and his foreman to Double X, and from there into town with Gibson, had not yet returned. The rest of the crew, with three exceptions, were busy skinning the cattle which had died in their plunge over the edge of the arroyo. Skinning cattle was hard, dirty work, but the hides would bring good money on the Kansas City market, and Nolan wasn't one to overlook a dollar.

Of the three who were left at headquarters, Lew Wong, the Chinese, was busy in the cookshack. Dakota Groves, who during the night had driven the cattle to their deaths, and thus missed his sleep, had stayed in his bunk until noon, and was now playing three card Monte with the twice wounded Ordway, whom Nolan was keeping out of sight until he decided what to do with him. Ordway was not a clever liar, and if called on to explain his first injury, might let it slip that the bullet had been fired by Dutch Schloemp.

Ordway was not clever at cards, either, and Groves soon cleaned him out, whereupon Ordway got up from the edge of the bunk on which he had been sitting, and stomped out of the bunkhouse. Not an amiable man at best, he was in an even uglier mood than usual after having lost a week's wages, particularly since he suspected that Groves had cheated. With two good arms he would have been no match for Groves, but he was planning his revenge as he entered the barn. So wrapped up was he in his thoughts that he was caught by surprise when Matt stepped out of a stall and warned, "Don't try for your gun or make any noise or the next bullet hole won't be in your arm."

Ordway, his mouth agape, stopped in midstride, and didn't move as Matt took away his six-shooter and shoved it inside his own belt. Ordway stared in fearful fascination at the muzzle of Matt's gun, and wasn't aware of Matt's question until Matt repeated it.

"Who else is here besides you? And don't lie, because I'll find out anyway."

With a visible effort, Ordway tore his gaze off the gun and looked at Matt. He motioned his lips with the tip of his tongue, and said huskily, "Just Dakota Groves and the cook. That's the truth, mister, so help me. For God's sake don't pull that trigger!"

"I won't," Matt said. "Provided you do exactly what I tell you to. Lie down on the floor, and put your hands behind your back."

Ordway dropped to his knees, then lay prone, but he said plaintively, "My arms ain't so good. I can't..."

"A little pain won't kill you," Matt said coldly. He had already decided that this was the man Dutch had wounded, one of the two who had set fire to the Schloemp barn and then killed Dutch. He placed a knee in the small of Ordway's back, holstered his own gun, and used his bandana to tie the man's wrists securely, ignoring Ordway's moans. With the wrists tied, he reached under Ordway to unbuckle his belt, and bound Ordway's ankles, after which he rolled him onto his back, and stood up.

"All right, Ordway, here's the situation. I'm convinced that you're one of the bastards who killed Dutch Schloemp, so the fact that you're in bad shape won't stop me from putting a bullet through you if you give me any trouble. You can bear that in mind when you answer my next question. This Dakota Groves you just mentioned, where is he?"

"In the bunkhouse," Ordway rasped. "My arms are killing me, mister. Can't you. . . "

"Consider yourself lucky," Matt said. "So long as your arms hurt, you'll know you're still alive." He reached down to yank Ordway's bandana out of his pocket, rolled him onto his stomach again, and used the bandana as a gag. Ordway was so thoroughly frightened that Matt believed he was telling the truth about there being only the three of them on the ranch, but it was a situation which could change at any minute. If nothing else, Groves could wonder what had happened to Ordway, and come looking for him. Matt hoisted the man onto his shoulder, carried him to a dark corner of the barn, and dumped him unceremoniously behind some bales of hay. He returned to the front of the barn and peered around the edge of the doorway.

The bunkhouse, as he remembered from his earlier visit, was some distance from the barn, and there was no way of approaching it except across a cleared space which offered no possibility of concealment. This left two possible courses of action. He could make a run for it, gambling on the element of surprise, or he could sit tight and hope that Groves would come looking for Ordway. And of course there was always the danger that some of the crew, either Nolan's bunch or the others, might ride in at any moment. This likelihood was enhanced by the fact that daylight was already fading.

Since the odds against catching Groves by surprise were so great, Matt chose the alternative. He went into a stall about halfway down the double row, and set himself to wait.

The time seemed to drag interminably, with nothing to show for it except that the daylight grew dimmer. Finally, when Matt's nerves were almost at the breaking point, a voice called irritably, "Ordway? What the hell are you doing out there?"

Silence. Then Groves again, and this time he sounded uneasy. "Ordway?"

Nothing was working out the way Matt had hoped. To begin with, he had come here for a showdown with Nolan. His plan, if you could call it that, had contemplated meeting Nolan alone. While he didn't doubt that Ordway and Groves were as guilty as their boss, Nolan was the real threat.

Well, it was too late to worry about that now. If Groves came to the barn looking for Ordway, it might be possible to get the drop on him, and perhaps force him to talk.

It soon became apparent that Groves was too wily to make a mistake like that. Instead of entering the barn, he circled the west side, his progress indicated by the jingling of his spurs. This sound ended abruptly, and Matt thought the man had stopped, but a ray of sunlight through a knot-hole in the side of the building was blacked out briefly, indicating that Groves had paused only long enough to take off his spurs.

Matt waited tensely, and for a long time nothing happened. Then he jerked as Groves called confidently, "I know you're in there, mister. I found your horse. Who the hell are you, and what've you done to Ordway?"

The advantage had swung to Groves's favor, and Matt knew it. All Groves had to do was wait for Matt to leave the barn. Or for Nolan or some of the Slash N crew to come back. Then there would be no escape.

If there was any chance at all, something had to be done before this happened. Matt faced the sound of Groves's voice, and called boldly, "If you want to know who I am, suppose you come in and find out. Unless you're scared, that is."

His answer was a jeering laugh, followed by, "It's no use, mister. I know what you're thinking. You figure that if. . ."

The voice broke off abruptly, and in the ensuing silence, Matt caught the sound of hoofs on hard dirt. Then Nolan called, "Groves?"

"Back here, boss," Groves yelled. "I've got a two-legged skunk cornered in the barn. I think he's killed Ordway. Better have the man spread out so he can't get away."

Nolan said something which Matt couldn't catch, but from the sounds which followed, it was evident that he had ordered his men to surround the barn. Then Nolan raised his voice and said smugly. "All right, Sheriff, you heard what my man said. There's a murderer holed up in the barn.

Since you're so great on law and order, suppose you go in and get him."

Matt was so shaken that he had to hold onto the side of the stall for a moment. The last thing he had wanted was to get the sheriff involved in this. What was the sheriff doing here on Slash N?

His question was partially answered when the sheriff called calmly, "I'm coming in, and I'm not armed. All I want to do is talk. Okay?"

If the sheriff wasn't armed, it could mean only one thing. He had been brought here against his will. So now Nolan had them both, and Matt knew that their chance of coming out alive was next to zero. But if he lived long enough to get off one shot, they would take Nolan with them. He took a deep breath, and called back, "It's me, Sheriff, Matt Dixon."

"I sort of figured as much," the sheriff said mildly, as he entered the barn. "I'm sorry I got you into this, Matt."

"Not your fault," Matt said, keeping his voice low enough so that those outside couldn't hear. "I'm curious as to how you got roped in, but Nolan isn't likely to give you time to explain. It isn't over yet, though, not while I've got bullets in my gun, and strength to pull a trigger." He raised his voice and called, "Nolan? Are you listening?"

"I'm listening," Nolan called. "Who the hell are you, anyway?"

"I'm the deputy," Matt called back. "I know you've hated me since the first time we met. Now's your chance to show that crew of yours how big a man you are. Come in and get me if you've got the nerve. Or do you always let somebody else do your dangerous work for you?"

"Why you damned whelp! I can handle ten of you. Just. . ."

"Hold it, boss," Groves cut in. "Let me finish this. After all, Ordway was a friend of mine."

Nolan didn't answer. Apparently he was relieved at this easy way out. After a bit, Groves went on. "We can't do much in the dark. Sheriff, there's a lantern hanging from a beam. Suppose you light it and then get out of the way. This is between your deputy and me."

"Do as he says, Sheriff," Matt urged. "I know what I'm doing."

Without arguing, the sheriff struck a match, located the lantern, and lit it. As he had said, his holster was empty. He looked at Matt, and there was something in the look that Matt couldn't fathom, but there was no time now for questions. Matt stepped out into the passageway between the two rows of stalls and faced the front of the barn. He was staking his life on the hope that Groves would be too proud of his reputation to shoot from darkness. His gamble paid off when Groves moved into the lamplight, a confident sneer on his face.

"So you want to be a hero. Or are you just too dumb to realize that you ain't got a chance against a real gunslinger?"

Matt paid scant attention to Groves's taunts. He was too intent on seeing Nolan. He had accepted the fact that he wouldn't walk out of this alive, but if he had time to get off one shot, it was Nolan he would aim at, not Groves.

Nolan finally came into sight, and Matt breathed a relieved sigh. He kept his eyes on Groves, and said coolly, "Any time you feel like it, mister."

Groves didn't move for a moment, but when he did, his hand was a blur. Something slammed into Matt's chest before his gun cleared leather. As he spun around and crashed to the ground, he realized that he had failed after all.

Dimly, he saw Groves raise his pistol for a finishing shot. Then the sheriff stepped into the line of fire, and Groves seemed confused. However, it was Nolan who spoke.

"What the hell's got into you, Sheriff? You're going to die, but you don't have to do it trying to save that damned deputy. Hell, he's nothing but a no-good drifter."

"He's not a drifter," the sheriff said. "He's my son."

Matt was growing weaker, but he was still conscious enough to make out the sheriff's words, although he couldn't at first believe them. Was the sheriff really. . .

Nolan laughed harshly.

"Your own brat! I'll be damned. This is practically made to order."

"What do you mean?" the sheriff asked, sounding puzzled.

"It's simple enough, Sheriff. Remember how you left me sitting at your desk while you went over to the restaurant for Gibson's supper? I opened one of the drawers, looking for a match, and saw that WANTED notice. The name Matt Dixon jumped right out at me."

"So what?" the sheriff demanded. "He's not wanted any more. Someone else confessed."

"Maybe so," Nolan admitted. "But the rest of it

still goes, the part about him swearing to kill his father. His father being you, as you just said. With the two of you dead, like you will be in a minute, I'll have no difficulty convincing folks that he found out who you were, and succeeded in making good his threat, but took one of your slugs in the process. I'll have plenty of witnesses to back me up." he gestured to Groves.

"Go ahead, man, get it over with."

Groves started to aim his pistol, but before it came into line there was the boom of a shotgun. The last thing Matt saw before he passed out was Groves crumpling to the ground, with Nolan falling limply on top of him. And the last voice he heard was Laura's, calling, "Don't any of you move! There's ten guns pointed at you!"

Chapter Twenty-Three

Laura's had been the last voice Matt had heard before losing consciousness, and it was the first when he came to. She seemed to be talking from a great distance, and he barely made out the words, "I believe he's awake, Doctor."

There were footsteps, and a man said briskly, "Let's have a look at him. Can you hear me, boy?"

Matt tried to answer, but the effort was too great, and he passed out again. Although he wouldn't know it until later, several more days elapsed while he hovered between life and death. Days during which he was dimly aware of being moved from time to time, and of having an arm under his shoulders propping him up while he was spoonfed something hot. Most of the time he just drifted and had crazy dreams, some of which were frightening, others peaceful. In most of the latter, Laura Gibson played an important role.

Finally there came a time when he opened his eyes and realized that he was in a bed. Not his bed in the hotel, for this one was soft and smooth, and the ceiling above him was not water-stained. He turned his head on the pillow, and saw sunlight streaming through a curtained window. Nothing about the room looked familiar.

He was too tired to expend any effort trying to figure out where he was. It was enough that he was alive and relatively comfortable. All he wanted to do was sleep, but apparently he was slept out, for sleep wouldn't come. Instead, his brain became more active, and bits of the past filtered through his mind, the Gunnison jail, that trading post near the Grand Canyon, Laura, someone pointing a gun at him, the sheriff. . .

As though a veil had been lifted, it all came back, right up to the point where Dakota Groves's bullet had torn into him. A little less clearly, he remembered the sheriff stepping between him and Groves. The sheriff's words came back. "He's not a drifter. He's my son."

Without thinking, Matt started to get out of bed. He managed to sit up, but the room began spinning around, and his head fell back on the pillow. Evidently he had made some slight noise, for there were quick steps, a door was opened, and Ellen Troup stood beside the bed. She had an anxious look on her face, but as he stared up at her in confusion, it changed to a relieved smile.

"So you've decided to rejoin the living. We were beginning to wonder. How do you feel?"

"Hungry," Matt said. It was the first word which came to his mind, and it surprised him as much as it did Ellen, who looked puzzled for a second, then began to laugh.

When she was able to speak, she said wryly, "For ten days you lie there like a mummy, and then the first thing you say is that you're hungry. Just like a man!"

"Ten days?" Matt exclaimed. "Good Lord, do

you mean you've been taking care of me all that time?"

"Oh, don't give me too much credit," Ellen said. "Laura Gibson has been sitting up with you almost every night. In case you're wondering, she doesn't go back and forth to the ranch daytimes, she's staying with some friends here in town. My goodness, I'm talking my head off, and you just told me you were hungry. I'll go out in the kitchen and get you some hot soup."

"Thanks," Matt said, and added uncertainly. "Do you mean this is your room I'm in? I didn't. . ."

"You shouldn't be talking so much," Ellen cautioned. "I'll be back in a few minutes."

So Laura had been at his side all those nights. The knowledge gave him a warm glow, although his elation was tempered with uneasiness. He hoped he hadn't been delirious, and said something he shouldn't. Maybe called her name?

His thoughts were interrupted by the re-opening of the door, only this time it wasn't Ellen who came in, but the sheriff. With a jolt, Matt reminded himself that he shouldn't think of him now as merely a sheriff; the man was his father, whom he had sworn to kill.

Evidently some of his mental turmoil was reflected in his expression, for the sheriff said quickly, "You don't have to say anything, Matt. I just wanted to see for myself that you were all right. I'll go tell Doc Yarborough you're conscious." He turned away and had reached the doorway before Matt found his voice.

"Wait! There's something I want to say. It won't hurt me to talk for a minute."

The sheriff hesitated briefly, then returned to the bedside.

"Go ahead and say it, Matt. It can't be any worse than what I've been telling myself for the last twenty years. You couldn't hate me any worse than I do."

"I don't hate you," Matt said. "Oh, I thought I did, and I've spent most of my life planning how to get even. But I can't do it any more. I think I started to change when that marshal up in Gunnison locked me in a cell. I would have gone crazy penned up like that. I felt the way you must have when you lit out. And then I found out that you knew who I was, and what I'd sworn to do, and still didn't turn me over to the law. Instead, you risked your own life twice, once in the courtroom, and again in Nolan's barn, to save mine. Good God! What a fool I've been!"

There were tears on the sheriff's cheeks, but he was smiling. Without speaking, he reached down to touch Matt's shoulder, then turned quickly and left the room, almost bumping into Ellen, who was carrying a big bowl of soup. She looked at Matt wonderingly.

"What in the world did you say to the sheriff? I've never seen him cry before."

"The sheriff?" Matt echoed, smiling. "Oh, you must mean my father. Nothing much. Are you going to let me have some of that soup, or do I just get to smell it?"

Laura Gibson, before leaving Matt's bedside earlier in the day, had elicited Ellen's promise to let her know when there was any change in Matt's condition, so it was only minutes before she found out that he was awake. She bathed and dressed as rapidly as possible, but although she almost ran to the cafe, she found him asleep again. The hot soup, combined with his general weakness, had prevented him from staying awake, even though he had been told that Laura was expected any moment. As a result, it was late afternoon when he opened his eyes and saw her sitting beside the bed.

She appeared to be asleep, and for several minutes he was content to worship in silence. Even in repose she looked tired, but to him she was more beautiful than ever.

It was she who broke the spell, opening her eyes and looking at him. The signs of weariness disappeared as if by magic, and a smile lit up her face.

"Welcome back, Matt. It's been a long time."

"Too long," Matt said. "Miss Troup tells me you've been watching over me almost every night. I don't know how to thank you."

"Then don't try," Laura suggested. "How do you feel?"

"Fine," Matt told her. "Well, maybe a little puny, but I'll be all right." He paused, then added haltingly. "Did I. . . did I give you much trouble. . . talk in my sleep or anything?"

"Not much," Laura said, but her face turned a little pink, and she quickly changed the subject. "I imagine you'd like to know what's happened since you were shot. Do you feel up to it now?"

Matt nodded, and Laura began.

"In the first place, both Nolan and that gunslinger of his are dead. No, it wasn't my gun that killed them. Lew Jennings fired the shot. If you heard me say there were ten of us, I was exaggerating a little. There were only eight: Mr. Jennings and his older boy, the three other ranchers, Will

Otis's hired hand, and Hank Debrow's boy, Link. By the way, we misjudged Hank Debrow. He didn't tip off Nolan about the meeting. We think it was Nels Nordquest's man, Liggett, because he left the country in a hurry."

"I'm glad it wasn't Debrow."

"So am I. Anyway, we found the man you had tied up. I believe his name is Ordway. He was so scared that he talked a blue streak. He and another man, Jeff Tyson, killed Dutch Schloemp and burned the barn, acting on Nolan's orders. We found Mr. Schloemp's horse in one of the Slash N sheds. Ordway claims it was Tyson who killed Dutch. He's probably lying, but there's no way of proving it, since Tyson has disappeared. So have almost all the Slash N crew except Dyke Blodgett, who took no part in the dirty work. He's hiring a new crew, and hopes to hold things together until some distant relative of Nolan's can be located back east." She frowned. "Am I tiring you?"

"No," Matt said. "But tell me about your father."

"Oh, Pa's fine. The sheriff turned him loose, of course, and he's out at the ranch, working like a beaver. He's hoping that when Nolan's relative shows up he'll sell us a piece of land on which Nolan outbid us last year. If we get it, he'll increase the size of the herd. Of course that will mean hiring a man to help out, but Pa says I shouldn't be doing man's work anyway."

"He's right," Matt said. "What you ought to do..."

"Yes?"

Matt didn't have the nerve to come right out and ask her to marry him. Instead, he said, "Have you ever been in Western Colorado?"

She looked at him curiously.

"No, but what does that have to do with anything?"

"I'll tell you later," Matt promised. "When I'm better able to defend myself. I'm glad things are working out so well."

"Thanks largely to you," Laura said. She reached out impulsively and touched his hand. "Ellen told me about you and the sheriff... I mean you and your father. I think it's marvelous."

Matt seized her hand, and she made no effort to pull away. Instead, she smiled and said happily, "Now that everything else is straightened out, I'm sure Ellen and your father will get married."

Matt frowned. The idea upset him at first. Then he thought about it some more, and the frown vanished. After all, it had been twenty years, and his mother had been dead almost two. He smiled.

"I'm glad to hear it. Pa couldn't find a better woman. If I were twenty years older, and she'd have me, I'd marry her myself. Except for one thing, that is; I've already set my sights on someone else."

This time there was no question about Laura's blush. Matt took her other hand and drew her face toward his, and at that inopportune moment the door opened and Doc Yarborough entered the room. Neither Matt nor Laura noticed him. He stared at them a second, grinned, and quietly let himself out. His patient was obviously well on the road to recovery.